USA TODAY bestselling and RITA® Award–winning author **Marie Ferrarella** has written more than two hundred and fifty books for Mills & Boon, some under the name Marie Nicole. Her romances are beloved by fans worldwide. Visit her website, marieferrarella.com.

Also by Marie Ferrarella

Matchmaking Mamas miniseries

Wish Upon a Matchmaker
Dating for Two
Diamond in the Ruff
Her Red-Carpet Romance
Coming Home for Christmas
Dr. Forget-Me-Not
Twice a Hero, Always Her Man
Meant to Be Mine
A Second Chance for the Single Dad
Christmastime Courtship
Engagement for Two
Adding Up to Family

**The Fortunes of Texas:
The Secret Fortunes miniseries**

Fortune's Second-Chance Cowboy

**The Montana Mavericks: The
Great Family Roundup miniseries**

The Maverick's Return

**The Fortunes of Texas:
The Rulebreakers miniseries**

The Fortune Most Likely To...

Discover more at millsandboon.co.uk.

The Cowboy's Lesson in Love

MARIE FERRARELLA

MILLS & BOON

First published in Great Britain 2019
by Mills & Boon, an imprint of HarperCollins*Publishers*
1 London Bridge Street, London, SE1 9GF

Large Print edition 2019

© 2018 Marie Rydzynski-Ferrarella

ISBN: 978-0-263-08334-7

MIX
Paper from
responsible sources
FSC
www.fsc.org FSC™ C007454

This book is produced from independently certified
FSC™ paper to ensure responsible forest management.
For more information visit www.harpercollins.co.uk/green.

Printed and bound in Great Britain
by CPI Group (UK) Ltd, Croydon, CR0 4YY

To
Glenda Howard,
With Gratitude
For
Continuing To Make
My Dreams
Come True

Prologue

"Are you nervous?"

Shania Stewart's softly voiced question to her twenty-six-year-old cousin broke through the otherwise early-morning silence within their small kitchen in their newly rented house located in Forever, Texas.

Wynona Chee didn't answer her immediately. She was tempted to nonchalantly toss her long, shining black hair over her shoulder and confidently deny the very idea of having even a drop of fear regarding whatever might lay ahead of her today.

Ahead of both of them, really.

But over the course of her young life, Wynona had gone through a great deal with Shania, more than so many women even twice their age. Always close, the cousins had suffered the loss of their parents almost simultaneously. For Wynona, it had been the death of her single mother—she had never known her father—when sickness and heartbreak had claimed her. For Shania, it had come in waves. First, her father had died when a drunk driver had hit his car, then her mother, who had by that time taken in an orphaned Wynona to live with them, had succumbed to pneumonia.

By the time Wynona was ten and Shania was eleven, they did not have a living parent between them. Instead, they faced the grim prospect of being sent off to family care where they would then be absorbed into the foster care system. The latter fact ultimately meant that they would be separated.

The immediate future that faced the two cousins had been beyond bleak at that point.

It was then that they learned the true meaning of the word *hope*. Their late grandmother's sister, Great-Aunt Naomi, came swooping into their lives from Houston like an unexpected twister sweeping across the prairie.

A fiercely independent woman, Naomi Blackwell, a dedicated physician who had never married, had been notified about the cousins' pending fate by the town's sheriff. She immediately came and took the girls under her wing and returned with them to Houston to live with her in her oversize mansion.

Over the course of the next sixteen years, Naomi not only provided them with a home, she also made sure that they both received an excellent education. This helped guarantee that they could go on to become anything they set their minds to.

It turned out that the girls had set their minds to return to Forever and give back a little of their good fortune to the community. After a short attempt to talk the cousins out of it, Naomi gave them her blessings and sent them off.

When they finally returned to Forever, the house where they had spent their early childhood—Shania's parents' house—was gone, destroyed in a fire some eight years ago. Some of the ashes were still there. Consequently, when they arrived back that summer, they moved into a house in town and then set about putting their mission into motion.

Today marked the beginning of their new careers. Shania had been hired to teach physics at Forever's high school while Wynona was taking over a position that had been vacated at the end of the school year by Ericka Hale, the woman who was retiring as Forever Elementary's second/third grade teacher.

"A little," Wynona finally admitted after pausing to take in a deep breath. She could feel her butterflies growing and multiplying in her stomach. "You?"

Shania smiled. As the older of the two, Shania had always felt it was up to her to set the example. But like Wynona, she couldn't be anything but truthful. It just wasn't in her nature.

"I'd like to say no," she told her cousin, "but that would be a lie." Her smile was slightly rueful. "I feel like everything inside me is vibrating to *Flight of the Bumblebee.*"

"Really?" Wynona asked, surprised to hear that her cousin was anything but confident.

She'd always projected that sort of an image. "But you've always been the calm one."

"Most of the time," Shania admitted. "But I'm not feeling very calm right now, although I guess I did manage to fool you," she told Wynona with a self-deprecating laugh. "Now I guess all I have to do is fool everyone else."

"That's easy enough," Wynona assured her cousin. "All you have to do is channel Great-Aunt Naomi." A fond smile curved her lips. "That woman could make a rock tremble in fear."

Shania laughed. "She could, couldn't she?" A wave of nostalgia came over her as she looked at her younger cousin. "Do you find yourself wishing we were back in Houston with her right now?"

"No," Wynona said honestly. She saw that her answer surprised her cousin. "Staying with Aunt Naomi would have meant taking the easy way. I think we both know that we're right where we're supposed to be just as I know that Aunt Naomi is proud of us for choosing to do this."

Shania smiled in response, nodding her head. "I think you're right." The young woman looked at her watch, then raised her eyes to meet Wynona's. She took in a deep breath. "Well, Wyn, it's almost seven. If we don't want to be late our first day of school, we really should get going."

Wynona nodded in agreement as she felt her butterflies go into high gear. "Okay, Shania. Let's do this."

Chapter One

Clint Washburn wiped the back of his wrist against his forehead while crouching down and holding the stallion's hoof still with his other hand. Seven thirty in the morning and it was already getting hot.

This was fall, he thought. It shouldn't be this hot, certainly not this early in the day. These days it felt as if things were making even less sense than usual.

A movement out of the corner of his eye

caught his attention. Clint frowned when he saw the skinny little figure entering the corral. After closing the gate, he was walking toward him.

Ryan.

The boy wasn't supposed to be here. He was supposed to be on his way to school by now.

Clint stopped working on the stallion's hoof. The tiny rock or whatever had worked its way under the horseshoe, causing the animal to limp, was just going to have to wait until he sent his son on his way.

He squinted. The sun was directly behind the boy, making Ryan's fine features as well as his expression momentarily difficult to see. Clint's frown deepened.

"Shouldn't you be on your way to school by now, boy?" Clint asked.

There was no warmth in his voice, only impatience.

Rather than answer immediately, the small boy looked at his father with wide eyes, his fine, light brown hair falling into his piercing blue eyes. He turned a slight shade of red before answering.

"I… I thought I'd stay home and help you with the horses today."

"You thought wrong," Clint replied flatly. "I don't need your help with the horses. That's what I've got Jake and your uncle Roy for," he reminded the boy crisply, referring to the ranch hand and his brother. "What you need to do is go to school." Shading his eyes, Clint scanned the area directly behind his son. "Lucia is probably looking for you right now. Don't give her any extra work," he instructed his son briskly, then ordered, "Go."

The answer, although not unexpected, was not the one his son was hoping for.

Summoning his courage, Ryan tried to change his father's mind. "But—"

"Now."

A stricken look came over Ryan's thin face. His shoulders were slumped as he turned on his heel and made his way back into the house.

"Kind of hard on the boy, aren't you, boss?" Jake Weatherbee asked. He'd waited until Ryan had left the corral and was out of earshot before he raised the question. "He just wanted to help."

"He just wanted to skip school, like any kid his age," Clint replied gruffly.

"So let him once in a while," Roy Washburn, Clint's younger brother, told him, adding his voice to the argument. "Nothing wrong with that. If you let your son work with you, he'll get to see just what it means to be a rancher. It's what Dad did."

Clint's expression hardened. This was not

advice he welcomed. "Dad didn't do any-thing. He was too drunk half the time to work the ranch. That's why *we* did. The boy has to learn discipline before he learns anything else, not to mention what they can teach him at school." Clint's eyes swept over the two men standing before him. "I want that kid to be able to pick his future, not be stuck with it the way you and I were," he told Roy.

Clint brushed his hands off on the back of his jeans. "Now, if you two bachelors are through debating whether or not I'm raising *my* son properly, maybe you can get back to doing what you're supposed to be doing."

"Didn't mean no disrespect, boss," Jake told him. "I was just remembering what it felt like being the boy's age."

Clint's eyes narrowed. "Maybe you should try remembering what it's like being your age and working for a living." He turned to look at his brother. "Same goes for you."

"Yes, sir," Roy answered with just a slight hint of mocking in his voice. He turned his attention back to the recently purchased stallion he was preparing to break.

Clint's frown appeared to have been chiseled into his features. He was more dissatisfied with his own behavior than with the behavior of either his brother or his ranch hand. He knew that ultimately, the men meant well even if he hadn't asked for or welcomed their opinions.

Clint blew out a breath. Maybe he'd gone a little too far. "Look, I didn't mean to go off like that," he told Jake and Roy. "I've got a lot on my mind right now and this thing with the boy isn't helping any."

Given a reprieve, Roy decided to take the opportunity to reach his brother. "Don't you think you're making more of this than you should, Clint? At least Ryan was offering to help. He wasn't just running off—"

"Yet," Clint interjected seriously. "But if I don't force him to do what he's supposed to, it's only going to get worse. I've got to nip this sort of behavior in the bud," he insisted. A distant look came into his eyes. It still haunted him. Seven years and the wound still hadn't healed. "I missed what was right in front of me once. I'm not going to let that happen again," he stated firmly.

Roy paused to look at his brother. Though Clint had shut down again, Roy could see the glimmer of pain in his eyes. He knew that he wasn't referring to his son when he talked about missing what was right in front of him. Clint was talking about Susan, Ryan's mother. He was talking about the bomb she had detonated in the center of his life.

He had come home late one evening to find a crying baby and a note pinned to the sheet in his crib. Susan was nowhere to be seen and he had no idea how long she had been gone. When it finally dawned on him that she wasn't home, he was absolutely devastated. The woman he adored and had been married to for almost two years had left without warning.

The short, terse note she'd left in her wake stated that she realized that she wasn't cut out to be a rancher's wife and even less to be a mother. She went on to tell him that he needed to cut his losses and forget about her.

According to her note, they had never been a proper "fit."

That had probably hurt most of all, the antiseptic words Susan had used to describe what to him had been the most wonderful part of his life.

What he had thought of as his salvation had turned into his personal hell.

From that moment on Clint had sealed himself off from everyone and everything.

He hired someone to care for his house and his son—in that order. He didn't feel that he was up to doing either for a long, long time. To keep from falling into an apathetic abyss, Clint forced himself to run the ranch and to look after the horses that he bought and sold as well as the cattle on the ranch. It gave him a purpose. Otherwise, he felt he had no reason to go on.

Time went on and he made peace with his lot, but he still didn't come around, still didn't reach out to the son who seemed to need so desperately to be acknowledged by him.

While no one could have accused Lucia of being an outspoken woman, his housekeeper did do her best to try to make Clint open up to the boy, but none of her efforts were successful.

Clint made sure that the boy was clothed and that he always had enough to eat, but that was where it ended. There was no actual bonding between them. If Clint did manage to make it home for a meal—which he missed with a fair amount of regularity—there was no animated conversation to be had at the table. If it weren't for Roy, who lived in the ranch house with them, there would have been very little conversation at all.

On a few occasions Ryan would try to have a conversation with his father, asking him questions or talking about something that had happened in school. Clint's responses usually came in the form of a grunt, or a monosyllabic answer that really said nothing at all.

It was clear that Clint didn't know how to talk to his son, or to people in general, for that matter. The wounds that Susan had left in his heart had cut unimaginably deep and refused to heal. Communication with Roy was generally about the ranch, while his communication with Lucia in regards to Ryan was usually kept to a basic minimum.

In essence, to the adults who dealt with him it was evident that Clint Washburn was in a prison of his own making. The fact that the prison had no visible walls made no difference.

No matter where he went, the prison he was in went with him.

This particular morning, when Ryan walked back into the kitchen after his father had rejected his offer to help with the horses, Lucia all but pounced on him.

"Where did you run off to?" she asked. The housekeeper, Lucia Ortiz, had made a clean sweep through the house already, looking for the boy who had been placed in her care from the time he was one year old. "If we don't leave for school right now, we're going to be late. Let's go."

Small, thin shoulders rose and fell as the boy followed Lucia out of the house to where her twelve-year-old car was waiting.

"I thought I'd help Dad with the horses," Ryan said in a small voice.

Lucia gave the boy a long look. "Did he ask for your help?" she asked, getting in behind the steering wheel.

Ryan scrambled into the passenger seat, then settled in. He buckled up before answering because he knew that was the proper thing to do.

"No," he murmured.

"Then why did you offer?" Lucia asked, talking to him the way she would to an adult rather than a child. The boy was going through so much; she didn't want to add to that by making him feel that he was being looked down upon. "You know your father has his own way of doing things. Besides, he has Jake and Roy helping him."

Ryan seemed to sink farther into his seat. His voice grew smaller. "That's what he said."

Lucia started up the car. It was getting late and if they didn't leave now, they really were going to be late. Glancing at the boy's expression, she could feel her heart going out to him. There were times that observing the awkwardness between father and son when they interacted was almost too painful.

"See," Lucia said, doing her best to sound cheerful. "You need to wait until he asks."

Ryan pressed his lips together, staring straight ahead. And then he raised his eyes to his ally. "What did I do, Lucia?"

"Do?" she questioned, not really sure what the boy was asking her.

Ryan nodded. "What did I do to make my father hate me?"

She was tempted to pull over and take the boy into her arms, but she knew that he wouldn't welcome that. He wanted to be treated like an adult, so she did her best to oblige. "Oh, *hijo*, he doesn't hate you."

"Well, he doesn't like me," Ryan insisted, hopelessness echoing in his voice.

"It's not that," Lucia insisted. "Your father just doesn't know how to talk to a little boy." *Or to anyone else*, she added silently.

"You do," Ryan said with feeling. "Can't you teach him?"

Lucia let her true feelings out for a moment. "Oh, *hijo*, if I only could. But your father is not the kind of man who would allow himself to be taught by anyone. He doesn't like to admit that he's wrong. He is a very, very sad man."

The expression on Ryan's face was equally sad. "Because my mother left. I know."

Lucia looked at the eight-year-old sharply, caught off guard by his response. "Who told you that?" she asked.

"Nobody," he answered truthfully. "I heard Jake and Uncle Roy talking about my mother, about how everything would have been different if she had stayed with my dad." The look on Ryan's face was all earnestness as he asked, "Did she go because of me? Is that why Dad doesn't like me?"

Not for the first time, Lucia had a strong desire to box her employer's ears. "Oh no, Ryan, no. She didn't leave because of you. Your mother left because she didn't want to live on the ranch. She wanted something more exciting in her life."

"More exciting than horses?" Ryan questioned, mystified that anyone could feel that way. He loved the horses as well as the cattle. Uncle Roy had taught him how to ride when he was barely old enough to walk. The horse had actually been a pony at the time, but it still counted as far as Ryan was concerned. He had loved being on a horse ever since that day.

Lucia looked at him sympathetically. "I'm afraid so."

Ryan just couldn't understand. "But what could be more exciting?" he asked, puzzled.

"That was what your mother wanted to find out." Lucia flashed a smile in the boy's direction. "She didn't realize that she was leaving behind the most exciting part of her life."

Ryan's eyebrows disappeared beneath the hair hanging over his forehead. "Dad?" he questioned.

Lucia bit back a laugh. The boy was absolutely and sweetly unassuming. "No, you."

Ryan frowned at the answer. He stared at the tips of his boots, waving his feet back and forth slightly. "I'm not exciting."

"Oh, but you are," Lucia assured him. "And you're only going to get more exciting the more you learn. For that," she pointed out, "I'm afraid that you're going to have to go to school. Do you understand what I'm saying to you?"

Ryan sighed and then nodded. "I guess so."

The housekeeper caught the hitch in his voice. "Ryan, you're not having any trouble at school, are you?" she asked, peering at his face.

Ryan shook his head. "No."

"None of the kids are picking on you, are they?" Lucia asked. "You can tell me if they are."

"No," he answered, then added quietly, "None of the kids even know I'm there."

Lucia tried something else. "How about your teacher? Do you like her?"

"Yes, I guess so." He shrugged again, then modified his answer. "She's okay."

Because she was trying to get the boy to open up to her, Lucia tried to encourage him to keep talking. "Why don't you tell me about her?"

Looking slightly bewildered, Ryan asked, "What do you want to know?"

Lucia thought for a moment. "Well, to begin with, what's your teacher's name?"

For the first time that morning, possibly that week, Lucia heard the small boy giggle. It was a charming sound, like a boy who adores his teacher.

He grinned as he answered, "Her name is Ms. Chee. She is Native American and used to live right here in Forever when she was a little girl."

"On the reservation?" Lucia asked the boy.

Ryan thought for a moment, as if checking the facts he had stored in his head. And then he shook his head. "No, she said she used to live in a house on the skirts of town."

"Outskirts?" Lucia tactfully suggested.

Ryan's small, angular face lit up. "Yeah, that's it. *Out*skirts. That's kind of a funny word."

"Yes, it is," Lucia readily agreed. She'd heard that the new second/third grade teacher had moved into a house in town. "Did Ms. Chee say why she didn't live there anymore?"

Ryan thought for a moment, then remembered. "Oh, yeah. She said when she came back to Forever, she found out that the house burned down a few years ago. She was sad when she talked about it."

Lucia tried to remember if she recalled hearing anything about a fire taking place near the town. And then a vague memory nudged her brain.

"Was Ms. Chee talking about the old Stewart house?" She remembered that the house had been empty for a number of years before a squatter had accidentally set fire to it while trying to keep warm. The wooden structure had gone up in no time flat. By the time the fire brigade had arrived, there was nothing really left to save.

Ryan nodded. "Uh-huh." He could see his school coming into view up ahead. Growing antsy, he shifted in his seat and began to move his feet back and forth again. "I think so."

Now that she had him talking, Lucia was loath to stop him. "What else did your teacher tell you?"

"She didn't tell me. She told the class," Ryan corrected her.

Lucia had noticed that the boy was very careful about making sure that all his facts were precisely stated. She nodded, accepting the revised narrative.

"Did Ms. Chee say anything else to the class?"

"She said lots of stuff," Ryan replied honestly. "She's the teacher."

Lucia tried not to laugh. "I meant anything more personal. Something about herself."

Ryan thought for a moment. "Just that she liked teaching."

"Well, that's a good thing." Lucia stopped the car right before the school's doors. "Now, go in and learn something."

"Yes, ma'am," Ryan replied dutifully as he slid out of the passenger seat and then closed the car door behind him.

Lucia watched him square his small shoulders before heading to the school's front door. She shook her head and then restarted the vehicle.

The boy had a lot of weight on his shoulders for one so young, she thought. He needed his father. She only wished she could make his father understand that.

Lucia blew out a breath as she began to drive back to the ranch. Maybe someday, she thought. Hopefully, before it was too late.

Chapter Two

Wynona smiled as she watched the children in her combined second/third grade class come trooping into the room. Seeing their bright, smiling faces as they walked in warmed her heart. It was like watching unharnessed energy entering.

Looking back, it was hard for her to believe that these same little people could have actually struck fear into her heart just a little more than a month ago. On the plus side, that feeling had passed quickly, vanishing like a vapor within the first few hours of the first day.

It was true what they said, Wynona thought. Kids *could* smell fear. Conversely, they could also detect when someone had an affinity for them, when that same someone really *enjoyed* their company and wasn't just pretending that they did.

Kids were a lot smarter than they were given credit for.

Her own class quickly realized that she was the genuine article. That she wasn't just saying that she cared about them; she really did. And when she told them that she wanted to make learning fun for them, they believed her, even though a few of them, mainly the older ones, had rolled their eyes and groaned a little.

Instead of calling those students out, Wynona sincerely asked them how she could make the experience more enjoyable for them.

Thanks to her approach, within a few days Wynona had a classroom full of students who looked forward to coming to school every day.

But as with everything, Wynona saw that there was an exception. One of her students behaved differently than the others. Ryan Washburn didn't seem as if he was having any fun.

Covertly observing him, she saw that he acted far more introverted than the other students. Whenever her class was on the playground, unless she deliberately goaded Ryan into participating with the rest of the class, the boy would quietly keep to himself, watching the other students instead of joining in whatever game they were all playing.

After watching him for a month, she had to admit that Ryan Washburn worried her.

When she talked to him, he was polite, respectful, but there was no question that he was still removed. The calls she'd placed to his home—apparently, there was only a father in the picture—had gone unanswered.

They were almost five weeks into the school year and she had placed four calls to the man. The man whose deep, rumbling voice she heard on his answering machine hadn't called back once, not even to leave a message. She was going to give the man a couple more days, she promised herself, and then…

And then she was going to have to try something a little more to the point, Wynona decided.

"Good morning, class," she said cheerfully as the last student, a dark-eyed girl named Tracey, came in. Wynona closed the door behind her.

"Good morning, Ms. Chee," her students

chorused back, their voices swelling and filling the room rather than sounding singsongy the way they had the first day of class after she had introduced herself.

Instead of sitting down at her desk, Wynona moved around to stand in front of it. She leaned her hip against the edge of the desk, assuming a comfortable position. Her eyes scanned the various students around the room. She was looking at a sea of upturned, smiling faces—all except for Ryan.

"Did you have a good weekend?" she asked them.

Some heads bobbed up and down while some of the more loquacious students in the class spoke up, answering her question with a resounding "Yes!"

Wynona slanted a look at Ryan. He'd neither nodded nor responded verbally. Instead, he just remained silent.

She hoped to be able to draw the boy out by trying to get her students to make their answers a little more specific.

"So, what did everybody do this weekend?" As some of the children began to respond, Wynona held her hand up, stopping the flow of raised voices blending in dissonance. "Why don't we go around the room and you can each tell the class what made this weekend special for you? Ian, would you like to start us off?" she asked, calling on the self-proclaimed class clown.

Ian, who at nine was already taller than everyone else in the class, was more than happy to oblige.

Wynona made sure to get her students to keep their answers short, or in Ian's case, at least under five minutes. She was careful to move sporadically around the room allowing enough children to answer first so that

Ryan would feel comfortable when it came to be his turn, or at least not uncomfortable, she amended. She didn't want the boy to feel that her attention was focused on him, even though in this case, it actually was.

After six children had each told the class what special thing they had done over the weekend, Wynona turned toward the boy who was the real reason behind this impromptu exercise.

"Ryan, what did you do that was fun this weekend?" she asked him.

When the boy looked up at her, she was struck by the thought that he resembled a deer that had been caught in headlights.

After a prolonged awkward silence, Ryan finally answered. "Nothing."

"Nothing?" she repeated, searching for a way to coax more words out of Ryan. "You must have done something," she said. When he said nothing in response, she tried again. "What did you do when you got up on Saturday morning?"

"I had breakfast," Ryan replied quietly.

There was some snickering from a couple of the students. Wynona immediately waved them into silence. "That's a perfectly good answer, Ryan. Everyone needs to take in a source of good fuel so that they'll have energy to do things properly. What did you do after you finished breakfast?" she asked patiently.

Ryan licked his lips nervously. "Chores," he finally answered.

"I'm sure your dad appreciated that you did those chores," Wynona told him with feeling. She looked at him encouragingly. "Anything else?" she coaxed.

The boy thought for a moment, as if trying to remember what it was that he did next. And then he finally mumbled, "I went for a ride on Nugget." Exhaling a breath, he stared down at the floor.

"Is Nugget your horse?" Wynona asked, hoping that might get him to talk a little more.

This time, instead of saying anything verbal, Ryan nodded.

There was color rising in his cheeks and Wynona realized that unlike the other children who all vied for her attention and were eager to talk, the attention she was giving Ryan just embarrassed him.

Wynona quickly put an end to his discomfort. "Well, that sounds like a really fun thing to do," she told him. "I loved going for a ride on my horse when I was your age. But I had to share Skyball with my cousin. Skyball was an old, abandoned horse that someone had left to die, but we saved it." She remembered that as one of the highlights of her less-than-happy childhood. Looking back at Ryan, she smiled at him. "Thank you for sharing that, Ryan. Rachel—" turning, she called out to another student "—how about you? What did you do this weekend?"

Rachel was more than happy to share the events of her weekend with the class.

As Rachel began her lively narrative, Wynona glanced back in Ryan's direction. She watched the boy almost physically withdraw into himself.

This wasn't right. She had to do something about it. Wynona was more determined than ever to get hold of Ryan's father and talk to the man. She wanted to make sure that Washburn was aware of the boy's shyness so they could work together in an effort to do something about it. She also wanted to make sure that Ryan's behavior wasn't the result of some sort of a problem that was going on at home.

* * *

When the recess bell rang and her class all but raced outdoors to immerse themselves in playing games they had created, Wynona quietly drew Ryan aside and asked if she could talk to him.

Instead of asking his teacher if he had done something wrong, or why he was being singled out, Ryan merely stood to the side and silently waited for her to begin talking.

She wanted to get him to relax, but she knew that wasn't going to be easy.

"Ryan, why don't you come and sit over here?" she suggested, pointing to a desk that was right at the front of the room.

Ryan looked at the desk warily, making no move to do as she said. He had a reason. "But that's Chris's desk."

"I know that, but I'm sure Chris wouldn't

mind if you sit there just for a few minutes. He's outside, playing," she reminded the boy.

After hesitating for another second, he finally walked over to the desk she had pointed out. Still hesitating, Ryan lowered himself into the seat as if he expected it to blow up at any moment.

Watching him, Wynona was more convinced than ever that there had to be something wrong, most likely in his home life. Was his father abusing the boy?

Taking care to make and keep eye contact as she spoke, she kept her voice as warm and friendly as she could as she began to talk to the boy.

"I know that I'm still new here at the school, Ryan, but I just wanted you to know that if you have something you need to talk about, or if there's something that's bothering you, no matter how small it might be, I'm here for you."

It was everything she could do not to put her arms around the boy and hold him to her. He looked so terribly vulnerable.

"You can tell me absolutely anything you want." She peered down into his face, trying her best to maintain that eye contact. The boy had attempted to look away, but she wouldn't let him. "Do you understand what I'm saying to you, Ryan?"

Ryan pressed his lips together and nodded, but he didn't say anything.

It was like pulling teeth, Wynona thought. Very elusive teeth.

But she was determined and she tried again. "Is there anything you want to tell me, Ryan?"

Ryan shook his head. "No, ma'am."

His answer was so low, she almost couldn't hear the boy.

She knew that she could only push so much without scaring him off.

"Okay, but if you change your mind," Wynona told the boy, "my offer still stands. And you know where to find me."

Ryan responded to her question in complete seriousness. "In school."

The corners of her mouth curved ever so slightly, but she managed not to laugh.

"Exactly." Wynona glanced at her watch. "You'd better get outside, Ryan. I've used up part of your recess playtime."

He obediently rose to his feet. "That's okay," he told her. "I wasn't going to play anyway."

Wynona took advantage of the opening, hoping to get a better understanding of what was going on in the boy's head.

"Why not? Don't you like to play, Ryan?"

She watched the small shoulders rise and fall in a helpless shrug. "Everybody already picked who they wanted on their side and what games they're gonna be playing," he told her.

She came to stand beside him, trying to convey in spirit that she was on his side. "Nothing's cast in stone, Ryan. There's always room for one more."

The look he gave her said that they both knew that wasn't true, at least not in his case. As he began to slip out of the classroom, Wynona called after him. "Would you like to help me put out the books for our reading lesson?"

Sensing that would only put him even further apart from the others, Ryan answered, "That's okay. I'll just go outside."

Watching him go, Wynona blew out a long breath. Granted, she hadn't been a teacher for all that long, but she could definitely recognize a cry for help when she saw it, even though none of those particular words had actually been spoken.

"Oh, Lord, what happened to you, Ryan?" she murmured under her breath as she observed the boy from the window as he made his way outside.

As she watched, Ryan went to a space on the playground that was totally devoid of any students. It was as if he had voluntarily placed himself in exile.

She needed to do something about this, Wynona thought. She honestly didn't know what, but there had to be *something* she could do. She couldn't just stand back and do nothing while she watched the little boy almost wither away and die on the vine.

Over the course of the next two days, Wynona attempted to call Clint Washburn three more times. Each time she called, the phone rang five times and then the call went to his answering machine. She already knew that she was calling a landline. Apparently, Clint Washburn didn't have a cell phone.

He also didn't answer his landline or check his messages, she thought, growing progressively more and more annoyed. Being annoyed was something rare and out of character for her but she was definitely getting there, she thought, frustrated.

When she "struck out" again, waiting in vain for the man to return any of her calls, Wynona made up her mind as to what she was going to do next.

She obtained Ryan's address from the administrative office—a closet of a space, she thought as she walked out—and drove over to Ryan's family ranch.

She knew that this was highly unorthodox, given that they were only entering into the second full month of the school year, but she was out of options. At this point she was dead set on giving Washburn a piece of her mind. She wasn't used to being ignored like this. Especially not when it came to a matter that concerned one of her students.

When she drove her vehicle up to the ranch house that afternoon, Ryan was the first to spot her. The sound of an approaching vehicle had already drawn him to the front window. He was looking out that window when the car pulled up.

The car was unfamiliar to him. The person emerging from it was not.

"It's Ms. Chee!" he all but shouted in surprise. Turning for a split second to look over his shoulder in Lucia's direction, Ryan repeated what he'd just seen. "Lucia, it's Ms. Chee! She's here. My teacher's here!"

Caught by surprise, Lucia quickly wiped her hands on her ever-present apron as she hurried toward the front door. Puzzled, she spared Ryan a glance. "Did she tell you she was coming?"

"No," he answered, his head moving from side to side like a metronome set on high. "She didn't say anything to me about coming here."

"Are you sure?" Lucia prodded. "Did you do something bad in school?"

Even as she asked the question, Lucia was certain that the answer was no. Ryan was the model of obedience at home, but nothing else occurred to her at the moment.

"No," Ryan answered in a small, uneasy voice that said he was wavering in his belief about his own innocence in the matter.

Lucia had reached the front door by now and began to open it.

"Well, she has to have a reason for this visit," Lucia insisted. The next moment the small, dynamic housekeeper was standing on the porch, a one-woman welcoming committee. "Hello, I'm Mr. Washburn's housekeeper, Lucia Ortiz."

Wynona quickly made her way up the steps to the housekeeper. She took the woman's outstretched hand, shaking it.

"Hello, I'm Ryan's teacher, Wynona Chee." She peered over the shorter woman's shoulder, looking into the house. "Is Mr. Washburn around?"

Lucia remained standing in the doorway, making no move to let the other woman in. Her first allegiance was to the family she worked for. "Yes."

Wynona had come this far; she was not about to back off or turn around and go back to town. "I'd like to see him, please."

"He's at the corral," Lucia informed Ryan's teacher politely. "But this is his busy season. He's breaking in the new horses."

From what she remembered, ranchers were always busy, Wynona thought. She hadn't come to discuss what the man was doing; she had come about his son, whose well-being was far more important than any horses or cattle.

"I'm sure that's all very important," she told the woman, "but what I have to say to him is far *more* important." She glanced over her shoulder. "Just point me in the right direction and I'll be out of your hair," she promised the housekeeper.

"Maybe you should wait in the house," Lucia tactfully suggested. "I can bring you some tea to drink. Or perhaps you'd rather leave a message for Mr. Washburn and he'll get in touch with you."

Right, because that had worked out so well, Wynona thought. "Sorry, but I did and he didn't so now we're past leaving messages and waiting politely. I need to speak to him now." She looked down at Ryan. "Ryan, can you take me to where your dad's working?"

Torn, it was the moment of truth for Ryan. Hesitating, he wavered for just a second and then he chose his side.

"Okay," he said, taking her hand. "Follow me."

Chapter Three

Taking a momentary break, Jake leaned against the corral fence. That was when he saw her, a tall, willowy woman with jet-black hair. She was dressed in jeans, boots and a work shirt. And she was heading straight for them.

"Hey, don't look now, boss, but from the looks of it, there's an angry lady coming your way," Jake alerted Clint. "And if you ask me, it looks like the lady's loaded for bear."

Roy was already looking in the woman's direction and she had his complete attention. "I don't care what she's loaded for as long as she brings it my way," Clint's brother declared wistfully. "Who *is* she?" he asked, intrigued. "I don't remember ever seeing her around before. I would have remembered that face," Roy assured his brother and the other man.

Jake hadn't taken his eyes off the woman since he'd first spotted her.

"Yeah, me, too." He glanced toward Clint, who was still working and hadn't bothered to look at the interloper. "You know her, boss?"

"Whoever she is, Clint, she's got your boy with her," Roy added, still not looking away.

"What the hell are you two going on about?" Clint demanded shortly.

He'd been up early, going between the stable and the corral, and working since before his son had gone off to school. He had only spared a minimum of time for the cattle today. He was in no mood for guessing games, or unannounced guests. He just wanted to finish what he was doing and get in out of the sun.

"I don't know about Jake, but I'm talking about the prettiest sight I've laid my eyes on in a long, long time," Roy answered.

Exasperated, Clint dropped what he was doing and finally looked up just as the angry-looking young woman stepped up to the fence. Rather than ducking between the slats the way he would have expected her to do, he saw her climb up and then over the fence, jumping down on the other side as if she'd been doing it all of her life.

He was aware that his son was taking all this in with awe. If he didn't know any better, he would have said that the boy had the makings of a crush on this woman.

"Which one of you is Clint Washburn?" Wynona asked, walking until she was right in the middle of them.

Clint noted that both his brother and Jake would have been more than willing to say they were, but since he was standing right there, they couldn't. Both looked in his direction.

"I am," he told her, taking off his work gloves and shoving them into his back pocket. "Can I help you?" he asked. His tone of voice clearly indicated that there were a great many other things he would have wanted to do first before turning his attention to whatever it was that this woman had come to see him about.

Wynona did a quick scrutiny of the man. He had broad shoulders and a small waist. His dirty-blond hair could have used a haircut, but it was his attitude that really needed work. The man was just as unfriendly as she had imagined he'd be.

"I'm Wynona Chee," she informed him, introducing herself. And then she added, "I'm Ryan's teacher," in case he hadn't listened to any of the multiple messages she'd left—which she was beginning to suspect he didn't.

"Well, Wynona Chee, if you're his teacher, why aren't you at school, going about your business?" Clint asked.

She resented the way he said that, but snapping at the man wasn't going to help Ryan and it was Ryan who was the important one here. So Wynona bit back a few choice words that instantly rose to her lips and kept her temper in check.

"I *am* going about my business," she informed him tersely, ignoring the other two men taking all this in. "Since you weren't returning any of the countless messages I left on your phone, I decided that a face-to-face meeting with you might be the better way to go."

"Oh, is that what you decided now?" Clint asked and she got the distinct impression that he was mocking her.

"Don't mind my brother," Roy said quickly, speaking up. "He gets kind of ornery when he's been working all day. Around here, whenever rattlesnakes take one look at him, they just head the other way."

Clint shot his younger brother a dirty look, which didn't seem to affect the other man at all.

Instead, Roy just shrugged in response. "I just thought she needed to be warned," the younger man told Clint.

At any other time, Wynona might have even been somewhat amused by this exchange between brothers, but she wasn't here to be amused. She was here because she felt that Ryan Washburn needed help in coming out of his shell before that shell wound up setting around the boy permanently, walling him off from everyone around him.

Wynona opened her mouth to state her purpose, then stopped. While Clint Washburn seemed uninterested in what she had to say, the other two men with him appeared to be all ears. She had a feeling that what she had to say wasn't something that Washburn would want the others to hear.

"Is there someplace we could speak privately?" Wynona asked Ryan's father.

Since he could see the woman wasn't going to just leave even if he didn't encourage her, Clint resigned himself to hearing her out about whatever minor, imagined complaint she had come to voice. It was the only way he figured he could get rid of her.

Gesturing around at the vast area surrounding them, he said, "Pick a place."

She felt that he was humoring her, but it didn't matter as long as he listened to what she had to say and, more important, took it to heart.

"How about over there?" she asked, pointing to the far end of the corral, away from the horses and the other two men.

Broad shoulders rose in a careless, disinterested shrug. "Works as well as any other place," he told her in an equally disinterested voice.

As she led the way to the spot she'd pointed out, Wynona noticed that Ryan fell into step right beside her. She didn't want to risk the boy overhearing his father saying something negative about him.

"No, you stay over there for now, Ryan," she instructed the boy gently.

"But you're gonna be talking about me,

aren't you?" Ryan asked. It was obvious that he felt that since this meeting was about him, he did have a right to be there.

She had a feeling that he was always being excluded, but this time it was in his best interest.

Wynona did her best to temper her answer. "I'd like to talk to your dad alone first, Ryan. When that's done, you can join us."

Because she took the time to explain this to him first, Ryan felt a little better about having to be left out. Nodding his head, he stopped walking and obligingly fell back.

His uncle came up behind him and put his hand on the boy's shoulder as Ryan's teacher and his dad kept walking. He waited until they were a little farther away.

"You getting into some kind of trouble?" Roy asked his nephew good-naturedly. He ruffled Ryan's hair with affection.

Ryan turned around to look up at him. "No, sir," he answered solemnly.

"No, I guess not," Roy laughed. "You wouldn't know trouble if you tripped over it." Ryan had always been a good kid, almost too good, Roy thought. A kid needed to get into things once in a while, but Ryan never did. "Why don't you come on back and help me and Jake get the bridle bits ready for those new horses?" he told his nephew.

He'd seen time and again how eager the boy was to help and for the life of him he couldn't understand why his brother kept turning a deaf ear to Ryan's offers. It just didn't seem right, he thought.

Both he and Clint had grown up working around the horses and doing every imaginable chore there was when it came to running the ranch. They'd practically been born in a saddle and it certainly hadn't done them any harm. It had come in handy when their father had totally stopped doing any work on the ranch at all.

Roy had told his brother more than once that working with the horses was good for the boy, but Clint never seemed to hear him.

He shook his head. If Clint kept this up, he was certain that his brother was going to drive a permanent wedge between himself and his son.

Roy certainly hoped that that young, pretty teacher had better luck talking some sense into his fool brother's head than he did, he thought, looking over toward where the two were standing.

With a shrug he caught up to his nephew and went to rejoin Jake.

"So what's so important that you felt you had to come all the way out here in person to tell me?" Clint asked once they finally stopped walking and Ryan's teacher had turned around to face him.

Wynona got right to it. Hands on her hips, she demanded, "Do you have any interest in your son?"

Clint felt his back going up instantly.

"What kind of a fool question is that?" he asked.

He'd raised his voice, but she wasn't about to be intimidated. "A pretty straightforward one as far as I can see."

His dark blue eyes narrowed. "Then maybe you have blinders on."

Wynona didn't take the bait, didn't get side-tracked by the hostility in his voice and she didn't get caught up in an argument. Instead, in a very calm voice, she told him, "I would still like an answer to my question."

His face darkened like storm clouds over the prairie. "Yes, I'm interested in my son."

She gave him the benefit of the doubt. "Then why didn't you return any of my phone calls?" she asked, her hands still fisted at her sides. "I told you I was concerned about Ryan's behavior."

What the hell was that supposed to mean? "Was he fighting?" Clint asked.

Responding to his tone, she raised her chin defensively. "No, but—"

"Was he failing finger-painting?" Clint asked her sarcastically.

Was he belittling education, or just her? In either case, she could feel her temper rising. "I don't teach finger-painting," she informed him.

The expression on his face was smug, as if he had just won his argument. "I figured that. Maybe you should."

What was that supposed to mean? Wynona wondered. In any case, she wanted answers out of him. She wanted him to verbalize what was going on in his head. "*What* did you figure?"

The smug look on his face didn't abate. "That you were just making lady noises."

"What?" She stared at him incredulously. "Lady noises?" Wynona repeated. What the hell was that—aside from denigrating?

Despite her best efforts, she could feel herself *really* losing her temper. Something about Clint Washburn made her want to double up her fists and punch him *hard*, knocking some sense into that thick head of his.

His attitude reminded her of a few men she had encountered as a student and growing up in two different communities: the reservation near Forever and Houston. More than one of her friends' fathers were painfully distant from their children, concerned only with their own needs. They never once realized the effect that their behavior had on their off-spring. She herself never knew her own father.

She hadn't known that there was any other way to behave until Shania's family had taken her in and she saw what a real father was really like. Dan Stewart had been kind and caring, taking care of her the same way he took care of Shania. Though she had known him only for a short time, the man had made all the difference in the world to her.

That was what she wanted for Ryan—before it was too late.

"Yeah. Lady noises," Clint repeated. "You come in, take one look around, unleash your emotions and think you've got the solution to everything. Well, you don't," he told her. "So, are we done here because I've got a ranch to run."

He was about to turn away but she caught his arm and made him turn back to face her.

"No, we are *not* done here," she informed him tersely. "Your son is starved for your attention," she said angrily.

He'd been surprised at the strength of her grip when she'd grabbed his arm. She was obviously not as delicate as she appeared. But that still didn't change the fact that she had no business telling him how to raise his son and he told her as much.

"I'm not going to coddle the kid."

"No one's telling you to coddle him," she retorted, her eyes all but flashing. "I'm just asking you to give him some of your time."

"In case you weren't listening," he informed her, getting to the end of his patience, "I've got a ranch to run."

"Then have him help you," she countered. She knew of a lot of kids who helped their fathers out on the ranch. Why was he being so stubborn about it? "And talk to him while he's helping."

Clint was getting really tired of having this woman tell him what she thought he should be doing with his son. "Look—"

She anticipated his protest. "Mr. Washburn, I'm not asking you to read bedtime stories to Ryan, although you might give that some thought—" Wynona couldn't help adding.

"You're kidding," he cried, stunned by her suggestion. Nobody read to him when he was a kid. That kind of thing wasn't important in his book.

"No, I'm not 'kidding,'" she told him. "But the point I'm trying to get across to you is that you need to take an interest, a *real* interest, in Ryan. Treat him like a person. Like he *matters*. Talk to him, ask him how he's doing in school, tell him about the things you did when you were his age—"

Clint cut her off. He didn't have time for this. "I don't remember," he snapped.

Wynona's eyes narrowed again as her frustration with this jackass of a man increased. It was obvious that he was stubbornly fighting her on this but she wasn't about to let him win.

"Then make it up!" she cried angrily. Catching herself, she got control of her temper. "The point is communication. Because right now, every day, this boy is slipping further and further away and if you don't try to stop that, to make him feel as if you care about him, he's not only going to wind up being lost to you, he's going to be lost to himself, too."

That sounded like a bunch of garbage to him. "That's your opinion."

"It would be yours, too," she informed him,

"if you just stopped and assessed the situation more closely like a father." She had almost said "like someone with a brain" but had stopped herself in time.

Clint waved her away and turned on his heel toward where Jake and Roy were waiting. "I don't have time for any of this psychobabble," he said as he walked away from her.

"It's not psychobabble," she insisted, calling after him. "It's common sense."

"Ha!" Clint countered, but he kept on walking.

He knew if he turned around to say anything more, she'd just drag him back into another argument and he had already wasted enough time on this woman and her crazy theory.

Clint kept walking until he got back to where Jake and his brother were working. Ryan was with them as well and the boy looked up at him the moment he drew closer. Before his son could say anything to him or ask any questions, Clint said, "Go into the house and do your homework."

"I already finished my homework, sir," Ryan told him quietly.

"Then go do something else," Clint ordered, turning back to what he'd been doing before that woman disrupted his day.

To his surprise, Ryan stood his ground.

"Can I help you?" he asked in the same small, hopeful voice he'd used the morning when he had asked the same question.

The word *no* hovered on Clint's tongue and he'd almost said it. But then he heard that teacher's vehicle as she apparently started it up and then began to drive away.

Good. The woman was really going back into town, Clint thought.

But what the woman had said annoyingly

refused to drive away with her. It seemed to linger in the air like a solid entity.

Clint frowned as he turned to look at his son.

"Yeah," Clint finally said, reluctantly relenting. "You can help—as long as you promise not to get in the way."

Stunned that his father had actually said he could help, Ryan looked at him, a wide smile spreading out over his small, angular face.

"I promise! Just tell me what to do and I'll do it, Dad," Ryan proclaimed eagerly. "Just tell me," he repeated.

Clint looked down at his son. Despite the boy's eager reaction, Clint couldn't shake the feeling that he had just unintentionally opened up Pandora's box.

Chapter Four

Hearing the front door open and then close again, Shania came out of the kitchen and into the living room. She smiled at her cousin. "You're home."

"What gave it away?" Wynona asked, dropping her purse and briefcase unceremoniously on the coffee table. She dropped herself down on the sofa almost at the same time. Anger had temporarily drained her.

The sarcastic remark was totally out of character for Wynona, Shania thought, so she didn't bother commenting on it.

Instead, she said, "You're usually here ahead of me. If you hadn't turned up soon, I was going to send the dogs out looking for you."

"We have dogs?" Wynona asked.

The sarcastic edge in her voice was beginning to fade. They didn't have dogs; they shared joint ownership of one dog, a German shepherd named Belle. Belle was more like a member of the family than a pet.

"Okay, 'dog,'" Shania corrected needlessly. "Belle likes to think of herself as a whole army." Because ignoring her cousin's obviously sour mood was not making it go away, she tried addressing it head-on. "Boy, you're certainly being unusually touchy tonight. Something go wrong today?"

Instead of pretending not to know what Shania was talking about, or denying her cousin's assessment, Wynona came clean.

"I tried to talk some sense into a knuckle-dragging blockhead, but I should have realized that my efforts were doomed from the start," Wynona complained. She closed her eyes, trying to center herself.

Coming farther into the room, Shania sat down on the sofa beside her cousin. "I take it we're not talking about one of your students."

Wynona opened her eyes and sat up, glancing at her cousin in confusion.

"My students?" she repeated. "I'd never say something like that about one of the students—"

"Then who are you talking about?" Shania asked.

"Ryan Washburn's father, Clint." Even as she said his name, Wynona frowned. "I went to talk to him today after school."

Shania hadn't heard her cousin mention the man's name before. Was that someone she'd known before they had moved to Houston with their great-aunt? "Why would you do that?"

Wynona's frown deepened. It was obvious she was struggling to get her temper under control. "Because the Neanderthal wouldn't return any of the twelve hundred messages I left on his phone."

Shania smiled. She was accustomed to her cousin's penchant for exaggeration. She didn't do it around anyone else, but Wynona felt comfortable around her and she relaxed the restrictions she imposed on herself when she was within earshot of other people.

"Twelve hundred?" Shania repeated. "That many times, huh?"

Wynona relented. "Okay, maybe it was more like eight."

Shania inclined her head. "A little more manageable number," she agreed. "What kind of messages were you leaving for this unresponsive parent?" she asked her cousin, trying to get a better picture of what had gone on.

"The kind of messages a concerned teacher leaves for the parent of one of her students," Wynona answered. She would have thought that Shania would just naturally assume that.

But Shania was still attempting to piece the story together. She couldn't remember seeing Wynona this angry or incensed before.

"One of the students getting into trouble and the father doesn't want to hear about it?" she asked, thinking of the most logical reason that would set off her cousin this way.

Wynona got up and, still agitated, began to pace around. "Oh, the father clearly didn't want to hear about it, but it wasn't because his son was getting in trouble." She swung around to face her cousin. "Oh, Shania, Ryan is such a sweet, sweet kid. If you saw his face, you'd think you were looking at an angel."

Shania was still feeling her way around this subject. "And he's not a little devil?"

"No!" Wynona cried defensively. "If anyone's a devil, it's that father of his." The moment the words were out of her mouth, Wynona knew she had gone over the line. She shrugged helplessly. "Maybe that's not exactly fair," she admitted.

Shania took her cousin's hand and pulled her back down onto the sofa next to her. "Wyn, why don't you take a deep breath and tell me about this from the beginning?" she suggested.

Belle chose that moment to come walking over to the two women. As if on cue, the German shepherd put her head in Wynona's lap.

"Better yet," Shania said, amending her initial instruction as she smiled at the dog, "Why don't you pet Belle and *then* start talking from the beginning?" She knew the animal had a calming effect on both of them, especially on Wynona.

Because she had never been able to resist the dog from the moment they had rescued the animal from a shelter literally hours before she was slated to be destroyed, Wynona ran her hand along the dog's back, petting her. The dog seemed to wiggle into the petting motion. A smile slowly emerged on Wynona's lips.

Watching her cousin, Shania asked, "You feel better now?"

Wynona was forced to nod. "It's hard to stay angry petting a dog."

"I had a feeling," Shania said. She remained where she was. "Okay, I'm listening. Why were you talking to a knuckle-dragging

Neanderthal and how did that wind up making you so late?"

Still petting Belle, Wynona answered the second part of that first. "I'm late because I didn't want to come home angry so I drove around for a while, trying to calm down."

That certainly hadn't worked out well, Shania thought. Out loud she said, "If this is 'calmed down,' I would have hated to have seen you the way you were before you 'calmed down,'" Shania commented. "I don't think I've ever seen you this worked up before."

Wynona could only shake her head, even as she continued to stroke Belle. "This guy just pushed all my buttons."

Well, this was something new, Shania thought in surprise.

"I didn't know you had 'buttons' to push. You were always the calm one," she pointed out. "So just what was there about this student's father that set you off this way?"

Wynona searched for a way that would make this clearer for her cousin. And then she thought of something.

"Shania, do you remember Scottie Fox's father?" she asked.

Hearing the man's name suddenly took her back over the years, to a time when neither of them was a decade old yet. Shania did her best not to shiver as an icy sensation ran down her spine.

"How could I forget?" she cried. "That man almost beat Scottie to death before Scottie's mother and grandfather pulled him off Scottie." The man's name suddenly came back to her. Henry Fox. "Later, Henry claimed that he didn't remember the incident at all. Is— Ryan, is it?" she asked, pausing as she tried to remember the name Wynona had just used.

Wynona nodded. "Ryan Washburn."

"Is Ryan's father like Scottie's was?" Shania asked, appalled.

That had been an extreme case. From what she could see, Ryan didn't have any visible bruises on his body and he had worn short-sleeved shirts.

"No, at least I haven't seen any evidence of any violence, but the man is just as distant, just as removed, as Henry Fox first seemed. Washburn showed more interest in his horses than he did in his son." Wynona looked at her cousin, a feeling of helplessness washing over her. She wanted to fix this. "That boy is starved for affection and attention."

"And you went to tell the dad that he needed to shape up and provide that for his son," Shania guessed.

It didn't take much of a stretch of the imagination for Shania to reach that conclusion. Wynona had always been a softhearted person.

"Well, what would you have done?" Wynona asked.

Shania sighed. With a surrendering shrug of her shoulders she said, "Probably the same thing that you tried to do, Wyn. But realistically, that doesn't change the fact that you realize that you can't change the world."

Wynona never liked being told what she couldn't do. And Great-Aunt Naomi had taught both her and Shania that they didn't have to accept limitations but to reach for the moon.

This, she thought, wasn't quite the moon. But in a way, it was more important.

"I just want Ryan's father to realize what he's losing if he doesn't do something about the way he treats his son," Wynona insisted.

Shania shook her head. "You know, Wyn,

I can almost see the words I'm saying to you just bouncing right off your head, never managing to get in."

"I hear you," Wynona protested.

"Okay, then you're just choosing to ignore what I'm saying," Shania guessed with a grin.

Wynona rose to her feet again. Belle fell into place right beside her. The animal was obviously anticipating food coming her way very soon.

"Let me start getting dinner ready," Wynona said, deliberately changing the subject.

Belle became even more animated at the sound of the word *dinner*.

"What makes you think I didn't start dinner?" Shania asked. She managed to keep a straight face as she asked the question.

Wynona slanted a look in her cousin's direction that practically said she had to be kidding.

"I know because the earth is still round and because the kitchen hasn't gone up in flames yet," Wynona pointed out.

"Very funny," Shania countered. "Well, maybe I didn't start making dinner because I know just how much you enjoy cooking and I didn't want to take that pleasure away from you."

For the first time since she had come home, Wynona laughed. "Okay, we'll go with that."

"Yes, we will," Shania agreed. "Unless you'd like me to return to our previous, unfinished discussion about you trying to single-handedly tilt at windmills and change the world."

Wynona blew out a breath. She had no interest in going back to that.

"You in the mood for chicken or beef?" she asked, going back to the topic of dinner because that was a far safer way to go than resurrecting the aforementioned discussion.

Shania flashed a smile as she looked at her cousin over her shoulder. "Surprise me."

"Okay, one surprise coming up," Wynona declared as she disappeared into the kitchen.

Belle was still following close behind, hoping for a treat—or five.

The truth of it was, Wynona thought as she worked in the kitchen, she welcomed making dinner. She needed something to focus on and cooking really did have a way of calming her. For her it was dealing with the familiar. Shania was perfectly willing to let her take over the kitchen. There was no competition between them, especially not when it came to cooking.

Shania had often said that her cousin could probably whip up better meals with her eyes closed than most people could poring over cookbooks and laboriously following recipes.

The ironic thing was that it had been her aunt, Shania's mother, who had taught her how to cook. Wynona's mother hadn't had a talent for it, but Shania's mother could make three-day-old dirt taste good and she passed on all her recipes, shortcuts and secret ingredients to her. She had been glad to do it when Shania had shown that she had absolutely no interest in cooking and certainly no talent for it.

Looking back now, it amazed Wynona how much she had managed to pick up in the short amount of time she had lived with her cousin and her aunt and uncle before the final tragedy struck.

And, just as in Belle's case, she thought as she put the finishing touches on the mashed potatoes, she and Shania had been just hours away from having their lives dramatically changed forever.

As it turned out, they did have their lives dramatically changed, but for the better, rather than what she and Shania had anticipated was going to happen to them. Their great-aunt had come sweeping in like a hurricane, scooping them up in her wake and bringing both of them to Houston with her. Dr. Naomi Stewart was not the most demonstrative of people, but there was no question in either Wynona's or Shania's mind that the woman had loved them.

That was what she was trying to obtain for Ryan, Wynona thought ruefully. She wanted the boy to feel loved, to *know* that he was loved. Despite what she'd said to Shania about the buttons that Washburn had managed to inadvertently push within her, she didn't think that the man was being remote because he didn't like the boy. She had a feeling that there was something else at play here. Maybe the man didn't know how to relate to his son—or possibly to anyone at all. Not out of spite, but because there was just something that kept him trapped within himself and unable to display any sort of feelings whatsoever.

"Well, if that's the case, Mr. Washburn, you'll be happy to know that help is on the way. Well, maybe not happy," Wynona amended, taking Washburn's disposition into account, "but it's on the way anyway." Finished with the mashed potatoes, she turned her attention to something else.

"Who are you talking to?" Shania asked, drawn by the sound of her cousin's voice and walking into the kitchen.

Startled, Wynona managed to recover quickly. "No one, just seeing how something sounds out loud. I'm working up a lesson plan," she said.

Shania crossed her arms before her chest and gave her cousin a penetrating, knowing look. "Why, Wynona Chee, I've never known you to lie before."

Wynona got her back up. "I'm not ly—okay, so maybe I was just talking to myself," she amended, backtracking.

Shania continued looking at her, waiting for more. "About?"

"Don't you have any lesson plans to work on?" Wynona asked her cousin, wanting to change the subject or at least put this one to rest. "Something else you should be doing instead of eavesdropping on me?"

Shania just continued standing there, smiling as she watched her cousin move about the cozy kitchen. "Nope. Even if I did have a lesson plan to work on, which I don't by the way, this is a lot more interesting." She tilted her head, giving no indication that she was about to leave the room or Wynona. "Something you'd like to share with the class, Wynona?" she asked.

Wynona just went on working. "No, as a matter of fact, I don't."

Shania didn't give up. She and Wynona were in tune to one another the way other cousins weren't. She had a feeling there was something more going on. Wynona had seemed too upset when she'd come home.

She tried another tack. "How about something to get off your conscience?"

"No, again." Wynona stopped moving around the kitchen and fixed a look at her cousin. "Look, Ryan's father just got to me and I'm trying to work that out. I'll be fine by the time we finish eating this meal," she said, nodding at the dinner she was busy preparing for the table.

Shania smiled. She knew when to prod and when to back off and stop pushing. This was one of the latter times. She smiled at Wynona. "You know, you just might have stumbled onto a new way to handle problems—cooking your way into working things through."

"Very funny," Wynona commented drily. And then she suggested, "Why don't you make yourself useful and set the table?"

Shania was more than willing to comply. "Well, if that's all it takes to be useful to you, you've got it. I'll go set the table."

"Shania," Wynona called after her.

The other woman stopped and turned away from the kitchen cabinet, holding two plates in her hands. "Yes?"

"Thanks."

Shania knew her cousin wasn't referring

to her setting the table. She smiled, nodded. "Don't mention it. My pleasure, Wyn. My pleasure."

Wynona laughed as she got back to preparing the chicken. "You certainly have a low threshold of pleasure, Shania."

"Well," Shania replied philosophically, "if you keep your expectations low, almost anything at all will turn out to be a nice surprise, guaranteed to make you happier than you'd thought you would be."

Wynona laughed, "Good philosophy, cousin."

"I always thought so," Shania said cheerfully. "Now, hurry up," she urged, taking out the silverware. "I'm hungry."

Chapter Five

Wynona didn't know exactly what to expect when she arrived at school the next day.

As had become her habit, she had come in early. Trying to take her mind off Ryan and all the different possible scenarios that might have taken place after she had left the Washburn ranch, she moved around the classroom, tidying things up and preparing for that day's lesson.

Despite moving at less than her regular

pace, she still found herself with a lot of time on her hands and nothing to do. When her students finally began coming in, she held her breath, watching the doorway.

But unlike other mornings, her attention wasn't focused on the children in her class. It was focused exclusively on Ryan, waiting for him to come in. There was a part of her, she had to admit, that was afraid that her visit to his ranch in order to have things out with his father had ultimately only made things worse for the introverted boy.

If that was the case, she would never forgive herself—after she went back to the man's ranch and boxed the man's ears.

But when the boy came in with the rest of his class and she saw the look on his face, she knew that at least for now, no return visit or boxing of ears was called for. Ryan was smiling, looking a great deal happier than she had ever seen him.

Rather than keeping his head down, Ryan actually made eye contact with her. And when he did, when he caught her looking at him, he smiled wider. It was as if the sun had suddenly come out, casting light on everything in the immediate vicinity right after a prolonged, heavy rain.

Wynona raised her eyebrows in a silent question and the boy's smile grew wider still. Breaking rank before he reached his desk, he came up to her and whispered, "I got to help my dad with the horses," and then just as abruptly he went to take his seat.

She hugged what he had just told her, dying to ask Ryan to elaborate. But she didn't want to embarrass the boy in front of the class by singling him out so she held off until recess.

It was possibly the longest two and a half hours she'd ever gone through.

Once her class began to file out into the school yard, she waited to see what Ryan would do. As she'd hoped, he hung back for a minute and then shyly, slowly, he made his way over to her. He moved like a newborn colt trying out his legs and learning how to stand for the first time.

Wynona waited patiently. "Is there something you'd like to talk to me about?" she asked, coaxing the words out of Ryan.

The boy's head bobbed up and down enthusiastically. Every part of him seemed so much more animated than it had been up until today.

"Uh-huh! My dad asked me to help with the horses!" he told her again.

Wynona's smile matched Ryan's. "Tell me everything," she encouraged. "What did you do?"

"I got to hold on to their bridles. Not all

at once," he said quickly, not wanting her to misunderstand. "I held on to the bridles one at a time."

As she felt everything inside her lighting up, Wynona nodded her approval.

"Very smart," she told him. "If you're holding on to more than one bridle at a time and the horses decide to go in two different directions, you have a problem," she said solemnly.

"Mostly I helped Uncle Roy," Ryan went on. "But at the end of the day, when we all went into the house, my dad said I did okay." He beamed as if his father had just paid him the highest compliment possible. His bright blue eyes were dancing.

It wasn't exactly an avalanche of praise, Wynona thought, but it definitely was a start. Most important, Ryan was happy about how things had gone.

She was careful to sound totally positive

about his experience. "That really sounds wonderful," she told the boy. "I'm sure you were a great help. How do you feel about it?"

"Wonderful!" Ryan declared. And then, although he had always been shy and withdrawn around her, Ryan threw his arms around her waist and hugged her, nonverbally expressing all the gratitude and joy he was feeling right at this moment.

After several minutes, he stepped back. "Okay if I go outside?"

"Absolutely," she told him with enthusiasm.

"See you later." Ryan waved as he dashed out into the school yard.

It's a start, Wynona thought. Moving to the side, she watched through the window as Ryan made his way outside where the younger students gathered to play. To her surprise, she saw Ryan approach one of the more quiet students. She obviously couldn't hear the few words that were exchanged, but she got the general gist as she watched the two boys begin to play together.

Definitely a start, Wynona thought as her heart swelled. She couldn't have felt happier than if someone had just told her she was in the running for the Nobel Prize.

Because she wanted Clint Washburn to know the positive effect his action had had on his son—after all, she had let him have it with both barrels when it had involved the negative effect he'd had on the boy—Wynona called Clint Washburn the first chance she got.

After five rings, the answering machine picked up.

She stifled a sigh and almost hung up the phone. But she forced herself to stay on until she heard the tone prompting her to leave a message.

"Mr. Washburn, this is Wynona Chee. Ryan's teacher," she added, then bit her lower lip because at this point the man damn well *knew* who she was. Washburn might be a lot of things but he wasn't an idiot. "I just wanted you to know that Ryan was like a changed boy today. He said you let him help with the horses. I can't begin to tell you how incredibly happy he was."

Every word sounded stilted to her ear. She couldn't seem to convey the really positive note she was attempting to express. She wasn't trying to pat herself on the back, and somehow, congratulating a father for acting like a decent father didn't seem right, either, but there was no way to state what was going on at school today without making it sound awkward.

Aware that she'd allowed several seconds of dead time to go by, she cleared her throat. "Anyway, I just wanted you to know. Bye," she said belatedly.

Hanging up, she realized that she had wound up repeating herself in the short message she had left on Washburn's answering machine.

With a sigh, Wynona returned the receiver to the cradle.

She had gotten her message across and that was all that counted. Maybe if Washburn was made aware of how far a little bit of kindness could go, he'd be more prone to act kindly toward the boy.

At any rate, she had done what she had set out to do. She'd let him know that his son had been a great deal happier today than she'd ever seen him and that was all she was trying to convey to the man.

Wynona forced herself to put the matter out

of her mind. Though she was happy about Ryan, he wasn't her only student. She had a classroom of kids to inspire and motivate and she needed to concentrate on them right now.

To her, that was the only way to learn—to turn everything into a stimulating, challenging game whether she was teaching the students math, or reading, or any of the other subjects that she touched on in her daily attempt to turn her students into eager little sponges soaking up the knowledge she was imparting.

At the end of the day, after all her students had cleared out of the classroom and gone to their homes, the euphoria Wynona had felt because of the way that Ryan had behaved was still there. She was still feeling pleased with herself.

She couldn't get over how Ryan's demeanor

had been so light, so different than anything she had previously witnessed from him. Wynona felt as if she could probably live off the fumes of that happiness for an entire month, if not more.

Sitting at her desk, she had just finished grading the surprise quiz that she had given today. It was a history quiz and as she reviewed the grades, she was pleased to see that most of the class had done very well.

She was even more pleased to see that Ryan had done far better than he normally did.

Though she knew all about the benefits of positive reinforcement, it still amazed her that a little bit of positive interaction with his father could have this much of an effect on the boy. It was as if he'd been trapped inside this dark box and all he had needed was this one simple act of thoughtfulness from his father to make him come out.

Wynona stared at the quiz she had just finished grading. Common sense would have dictated that she just hand the quiz back to Ryan tomorrow when she gave the rest of the students back their quizzes.

But right now she felt this strong urge to show Washburn what a little bit of kindness and attention on his part had managed to accomplish in his son's case. Most of all, she secretly hoped that this would encourage the man to continue treating his son this way.

She pressed her lips together as she went on looking at the quiz.

"Let it go, Wynona. Nobody's paying you to be this man's conscience," she murmured under her breath. "Most likely, he'll probably resent you for it. You know what bullheaded men are like."

She wavered over the matter, her good intentions warring with her common sense.

In the end, her common sense never had a chance. Her desire to make sure that Washburn's actions had not been just a one-time thing, or a fluke that the rancher had committed in a moment of what the man would probably think of as weakness, had Wynona making up her mind on what course of action to take.

For the second time in two days, she drove to the Washburn ranch.

This time, when she arrived, Wynona didn't stop at the ranch house first. On a hunch, she drove her small, fifteen-year-old car toward where she had seen the corral yesterday.

Not wanting to risk spooking the horses just in case Washburn and his hands were working with the animals in the corral, she parked her vehicle about a quarter of a mile away from it.

As she made her way toward the corral, Wynona could immediately make out Washburn. The two other men she had seen working alongside the rancher were with him, as well.

The person she didn't see in the area was the one person she was actually looking for. Ryan was nowhere around.

Her heart dropped.

The next moment Wynona forced herself to rally. She'd been right in coming out, she told herself. This man not only had to be led to water, he also had to be tethered next to the stream and forcibly have his muzzle held right in the water.

As with the first time, Washburn wasn't the first to see her. He was too busy working with one of the horses. It was his brother, Roy, who saw her first.

Roy stopped what he was doing to admire

the figure Ryan's teacher cut as she strode toward the corral and them.

"What did you do wrong this time, Clint?" he asked his brother.

Clint didn't even bother looking up. If he stopped every time one of the other two men felt like talking, he'd told them that he would never be able to get anything done.

So instead, he growled, "What the hell are you talking about?"

Not waiting for an answer, Roy just continued talking. He'd already made an assumption. "Whatever it was, it brought that spitfire of a teacher back, big brother," Roy told him.

Clint didn't have to look at his brother to know that he was grinning ear to ear. He could hear it in Roy's voice.

With a sigh, he looked over in the direction of the ranch house. That was when he saw her. Ryan's teacher, heading straight for them.

For him.

Just like yesterday. It was almost like déjà vu, except that the woman was wearing different clothes than she had yesterday.

He noticed the way she moved in them.

He noticed everything about her.

Muttering under his breath, Clint took off his gloves and dropped them as he headed toward the woman. *Now what?* he wondered, annoyed.

"Need backup?" Jake asked, calling after Clint as the latter strode toward the teacher.

"No," Clint bit off. "You just keep on working," he ordered the ranch hand.

Never taking his eyes off the woman—it both impressed and annoyed him that she met his glare head-on—he cut the distance between them until they were finally facing each other.

"Something else on your mind, *Ms.* Chee?" he asked.

Wynona unconsciously squared her shoulders, bracing herself for a no-holds-barred confrontation. Her eyes continued to meet his.

"Yes," she informed him. "I came to tell you that Ryan has gotten a ten on his quiz."

"A ten?" Clint repeated. He knew his son wasn't a walking brain, but the kid wasn't dumb, either. "That doesn't sound very good."

"That's ten out of ten," Wynona pressed, realizing that Washburn probably thought she meant ten out of a hundred.

The angry crease across his forehead relaxed. "All right, then that's a good grade."

"Yes, it is." For just a split second, Wynona caught herself being distracted by Washburn's chiseled face. There was such a thing as being too good-looking. And this man was. "And I also came to tell you that Ryan was like a different boy in class today. He was actually smiling."

Clint continued to peer intently at her. "And you think that's a good thing?"

Did he actually have to be told that? she couldn't help wondering. "Yes," she said emphatically. "That's a good thing."

"Okay," Clint said, trying to get to the bottom of why she'd appeared on his property and came at him as if she wanted to hang him by his thumbs. "So why do you look like lightning bolts are about to come shooting out of your eyes?"

The rancher was more than six inches taller than she was but Wynona wasn't about to be intimidated or back down. This was important. "Because you obviously thought that treating Ryan like a human being was a one-time thing and you and I both know that it can't be."

He stared at her. "Let me get this straight. You came all the way out here so that you could lecture me again?" he demanded.

Honey. She could catch more flies with honey, she silently cautioned herself. Wynona tempered her voice. "I'm not here to lecture," she answered in a softer voice. "I'm here to beg you."

Clint's eyes narrowed as he continued to pin her in place. "I don't follow."

"Then let me explain." She noted that Ryan's father bristled slightly at her tone. She proceeded carefully. "That little bit of attention you showed your son had a huge effect on him. For the first time since the beginning of the school year, I saw a smile on Ryan's face. Not only that, but come recess time, he actually went out to play on the playground," she told him.

To her surprise, Washburn looked completely unimpressed. "I thought he was supposed to learn something, not play."

"Part of learning is to learn how to play with others," Wynona countered. "My job isn't just to teach reading, math and history," she told him, her voice beginning to rise. "My job is to teach the whole child, to help him cope as he goes on to be a well-adjusted adult."

A look of impatience creased Clint's face. "Adult? He's eight."

"But he's not *always* going to be eight," Wynona reminded him.

Clint made the natural progression. "Nine's not an adult, either."

"No, but it's closer to an adult than eight. See how this goes?" she asked.

He'd wasted enough time arguing with this woman. "What I'd like to see going is you, Ms. Chee, because I have work to do."

He began walking away from her. She was

quick to catch up. She wasn't finished with him yet. "Seems like you always have work to do."

"You're catching on," he tossed over his shoulder as he kept on walking.

"Your number-one priority should be your son," Wynona insisted, following him again.

Clint stopped walking and turned to face her, annoyed. "I don't need you to tell me that."

But Wynona didn't back down. "I think you do."

"Don't take this the wrong way," he began, "but I don't really care what you think."

She surprised him by saying, "Fair enough— but don't you care what your son thinks?"

He didn't answer her, but a small voice behind her spoke up. "Ms. Chee, what are you doing here?" Ryan asked.

Turning around, she saw that Ryan was

standing right behind her. She hadn't even heard the boy come up.

"I, um, came to show your father your quiz." She pulled the paper out of her bag and held it up for the little boy to see it. "You got a ten, Ryan. I'm very proud of you."

Ryan took the paper in his hands, his eyes shining. "I got a ten?" he cried, and then he grinned. "Hey, I did. I got them all right!" It was obvious that he was thrilled. He looked up at his teacher and then at his father. "I'm gonna go put this back in the house. Is that okay, Dad?"

Clint nodded. "Yeah, sure. That's fine."

Ryan was almost jumping up and down. "And then I'll come right back to help you like you said you wanted me to."

As she watched the boy dash off, Ryan's joyfully proclaimed words replayed themselves in her head. Washburn had actually asked the boy to help. Just as she had told him he should do. Apparently, the rancher was one jump ahead of her.

More than a little embarrassed, Wynona turned to look at the boy's father.

She cleared her throat and then said, "I guess I owe you an apology."

Chapter Six

Clint allowed his eyes to drift slowly over the length of the woman standing in front of him. He didn't say anything. It was as if he was taking stock of his words, deciding which ones he was going to use. Seconds went by, intensifying the silence.

Finally, he acknowledged, "I guess maybe you do after jumping all over me like that."

By then Roy had obviously decided to join them. He was as curious about things as his older brother seemed to be indifferent to them. Roy had managed to reach his brother and Ryan's teacher just in time to hear the last exchange.

The younger Washburn filled in whatever blanks still existed. "C'mon, Clint, lighten up. Ms. Chee wasn't trying to tread on your toes. She was just thinking of the boy and putting his best interests before everything else."

"I was," Wynona said, quick to pick up the lifeline. "But obviously I spoke out of turn because I wound up jumping to conclusions. The wrong conclusions," she emphasized. "After seeing Ryan so happy earlier today, when I came out here just now, it looked like he'd been excluded from the activity that meant so much to him, so I thought—well, I guess you can see why I thought what I did." She looked at him, expecting Washburn to come to the same conclusion that she had.

"Actually, no, I can't," Clint answered flatly. "Maybe because I'm not in the habit of sticking my nose into other people's business."

"Clint!" Roy's admonishment came automatically before he had a chance to censor himself.

Although he was definitely on her side, Wynona hardly took note of Washburn's brother. She was entirely focused on Ryan's father—and doing her best not to lose her temper. Again.

The man had definitely cornered the market in pigheadedness, she thought.

"Your son's welfare *is* my business, in the same way that the welfare of all the other children in my care is my business," she informed Clint icily. Her eyes had narrowed into slits and she had raised her chin pugnaciously.

"Did I miss something here?" Clint demanded. "Aren't you Ryan's teacher, not his social worker?"

The man looked as if he was on the verge of having steam come out of his ears, but she wasn't about to allow him to intimidate her. Angry, she was not about to back off. "We're all our brother's keeper."

"Oh wow, lady. You really are something else, you know that?" Washburn marveled and she didn't have to guess that he didn't mean that in a flattering way.

Shooting Clint an impatient look, Roy took a step forward, moving closer to his nephew's teacher. "I'd like to apologize for my brother."

Clint's dark look shifted toward his brother. "Nobody asked you to speak for me," he informed Roy coldly.

The last thing she wanted was to start something between Ryan's father and his uncle. "That's all right, I should be—"

"Dad," Ryan called out as he returned from the house. "Lucia wants to know if Ms. Chee is gonna stay for dinner. Can she?"

Both Clint and Wynona turned toward the boy and answered his question almost at the same time.

"No!"

And, at the same time, they both saw the boy's face as it fell.

Seeing his obvious disappointment, Wynona felt a sharp stabbing pain in her heart. However, despite the housekeeper's question, she was not about to stay anywhere she wasn't welcomed. It didn't take any sort of advanced degree for her to see that she definitely wasn't welcomed at Clint Washburn's table.

Clint's expression didn't change when he saw the distressed look on his son's face, but that didn't mean that he was unaffected by it. Although he had managed, over the years, to build an almost airtight wall around himself, sometimes that wall got a little fissure and just for a moment, feelings would get through.

Wanting to just drop the matter, for some reason he couldn't begin to fathom, Clint felt compelled to offer a halfhearted explanation to his son. "Ms. Chee's too busy to have dinner with us."

Rather than accept his father's explanation, Ryan looked up at his teacher as if he harbored a slim hope that she would change her mind if he pressed her to explain why she couldn't come.

"Are you really too busy, Ms. Chee?" Ryan asked her.

The wound in her heart grew a little larger. Wynona could easily see having her stay for dinner meant a lot to the boy and although she would have rather walked barefoot over hot coals than break bread with Clint Washburn, he wasn't the one who mattered here.

And neither was she.

Only Ryan mattered and for him, she *would* break bread with his father as long as doing so would bring back that sweet smile to the boy's small face.

Bracing herself for what she knew in her heart was going to be an ordeal, she asked Ryan, "What time's dinner?"

Wynona deliberately avoided his father's penetrating stare.

"Five o'clock," Ryan announced, almost singing out the words. The hopeful look on his face had doubled as he asked again, "Can you stay, Ms. Chee?"

"Well," she replied, this time looking over Ryan's head at his father, "I wouldn't want to intrude where I'm not wanted."

The ball was now in Washburn's corral, she thought, waiting for him to say something.

Clint laughed shortly. "Well, that pony's already ridden out of town," he informed her evenly.

"What my brother's trying to say in his own special way is that of course you're welcome," Roy said, a broad smile on his handsome face. "We'd be honored to have you join us for dinner."

It wasn't easy, but Wynona managed not to laugh. "I don't think that's quite the word that Ryan's dad is thinking right now," Wynona responded. She was talking to Roy but it was obvious that she was looking at his brother.

The corners of Clint's mouth curved ever so slightly in a smile that only had a vague hint of humor underlining it.

"So now you're a mind reader?" Clint asked her.

Wynona's eyes met his. She never wavered.

"Doesn't take much reading in this case," she answered.

For his son's sake, Clint preferred to think that the woman was saying his feelings were obvious rather than saying that he was just simpleminded.

Looking at Ryan, he said, "Why don't you take your teacher into the house and keep her company until we're finished out here?"

Ryan looked almost stricken. "But I thought I was going to help you fix the fence," he protested.

Wynona immediately picked up on the boy's distress. "I don't want to disrupt anything," she protested. And then an idea occurred to her. "As a matter of fact, why don't you let me help?" She looked at Clint. "That way you can get finished that much sooner."

"Help?" Clint echoed incredulously. Was she kidding? Okay, so she could climb over a fence better than he would have thought, but now they were talking about basic labor. And the teacher had delicate hands.

"This is the kind of work where you have to get your hands dirty," he told her as if that alone would have her turning on her heel and quickly retreating into the ranch house.

She chalked his insult up to the fact that Washburn wasn't very good at sizing up people. "I'm familiar with work on a ranch, Mr. Washburn," she told him with a smile she didn't feel. "I grew up on one."

Clint looked at her skeptically, but he decided to call her bluff. "All right, pick up a hammer and make yourself useful." He looked at his brother. Since Roy seemed to have appointed himself this woman's champion, he could work with her. "Roy, take her with you and go work on that length of rotting fence over there," he said, indicating the break that they had discovered earlier in the day.

"Sure thing," Roy agreed. He looked more than happy to comply. It was obvious that the thought of having Wynona accompany him while he worked on the length of fence that needed replacing had just brightened his afternoon.

"Don't worry," Roy told her, lowering his voice as they began to walk away. "I won't really put you to work."

"I'm not worried," Wynona told him as she followed Washburn's younger brother to the section that Washburn had just pointed to. "But I think you missed the point. I offered to help to make the work go faster. I meant that. I don't say things I don't mean."

He couldn't picture her swinging a hammer or using a saw. "Then you weren't just saying that for Clint's benefit? Not that I'd blame you," he said quickly. "My brother's got a knack of really rubbing most people the wrong way," Roy confessed. He stopped in front of a section of fencing that was clearly in need of work. Picking up a hammer, he began removing planks of rotting wood. "But he wasn't always that way."

"Nice to know," Wynona commented.

She wasn't really in the mood to listen to Roy make excuses for his brother, even though that did speak well of the younger man. Spotting a second, discarded hammer on the ground, she got to work herself.

Roy watched her out of the corner of his eye, surprised and amazed. She worked like someone who was used to working with her hands and who could assess what needed to be done without waiting for directions.

He grinned at her. "You really did work on a ranch, didn't you?"

Responding, Wynona grinned back. "I told you I don't lie," she said with a wink. "Now, let's put some muscle into this and see if we can't get finished mending this length of fence before your brother finishes his."

"A competition, huh?" Roy asked. "Well, you won't get an argument out of me," he told her. Roy stepped up his pace.

Pausing just for a moment, Clint watched his brother and Ryan's teacher working from across the field. The next moment he roused himself and got back to work with Jake as Ryan hovered about, eager to assist in any way he could.

Glancing back across the field, Clint had to admire the woman's tenacity, not to mention her form. From where he was standing, there was something almost hypnotic about the way she swung her hammer and threw herself into her work.

Well, she wasn't afraid of getting dirty, he'd give her that, Clint thought grudgingly. Quite honestly, for the first fifteen minutes he kept waiting for her to throw down her hammer, declare that she was suddenly really tired and walk away from the fence.

But she didn't walk away, didn't stop. She just kept on working and though he hated to admit it, she was actually pretty good at it.

Maybe even better than pretty good, Clint admitted grudgingly, although he made the silent admission only to himself. He wouldn't have said anything of the kind to anyone out loud.

Apparently, he didn't have to, he realized. Ryan was more than happy to make the proclamation for him and anyone else within earshot.

"I didn't know Ms. Chee could fix things," his son said in awe as he looked over to where his teacher was working with his uncle. "I guess she can do just about anything, huh, Dad?"

He wasn't about to validate that sentiment, or to say anything more about the teacher than he absolutely had to. "Hold that steadier," Clint instructed, nodding at the post his son had his small hands on. He'd already anchored the post in the ground. All that was left were the final swings. "I don't want to hit your head by mistake."

"No, sir, I don't want that, either," Ryan answered, turning his attention back to the pole he was holding for his father.

"That's better," Clint commented.

In reality, there was no danger to the boy. He'd safeguarded the pole before he had let Ryan near it. He was allowing Ryan to think he was holding it upright while he drove it into the ground with a sledgehammer so that the boy would feel part of this since it seemed to mean so much to him—as well as to that busybody teacher of his, Clint thought, casting another glance in the woman's direction.

Why the woman felt called upon to horn into his life was totally beyond him. No matter what explanations she spouted, as far as he was concerned it wasn't right for her to come on out here, looking in on him to make sure he was treating his son well.

She didn't know him. The woman had no reason to believe that he had, or ever would, mistreat the boy.

Like he'd ever hurt Ryan, Clint thought angrily. He wasn't that kind of man. But neither was he the kind of man who coddled his son, either. That was against everything he believed in.

Still, he supposed that it wouldn't hurt to teach the boy a few of the basic things, show him how they were done so that he could make himself useful once he got older and actually could be put to work.

Clint slanted another look toward the teacher.

He was more than able to raise his own son without having that woman coming to the ranch to "share her wisdom" with him. Who the hell did she think she was anyway?

"Did I do something wrong, Dad?"

The small, hesitant voice broke through Clint's thoughts, forcing him to push them aside. Replaying Ryan's words, Clint looked down to see that his son was looking at him with wide, fearful eyes.

"Why would you think that?" he asked.

"'Cause you have on your mad face," Ryan answered nervously.

Looking over toward him, Jake nodded. "You do, you know," the ranch hand said.

What the hell was going on today? "What

are you talking about?" Clint asked. "Has everyone gone crazy today?"

"If I had a mirror with me, I'd hold it up and show you," Jake told him. "But I don't, so you're just going to have to take it from me. You're scary. Nobody can scowl the way you do, boss. Very effective," Jake commented. "Guaranteed to put the fear of God into all of us when you look like that."

Clint started to say that they were both imagining things but then he stopped. To be honest, he could feel the muscles in his jaw tightening. They only did that when he was scowling.

He took a long breath, then forced himself to relax. It wasn't easy. He'd been so intense for so long that the expression he was being accused of wearing came naturally to him and it wasn't easy just to banish it.

But Clint had no intention of allowing Ryan's teacher to feel that she had somehow bested him, making him do something he hadn't wanted to. Concentrating, he pulled his lips back until they appeared to approximate a smile. His eyes met Jake's.

The latter held up his hands, pretending to take a step back. "That's even worse," he retorted. "Maybe you should go back to scowling."

"No, he shouldn't," Ryan cried, speaking up. He turned toward his father. "You look nice when you smile, Dad. Like you're happy."

"Like a rattler just before he strikes," Jake murmured.

"Rattlesnakes don't smile," Ryan protested, distressed. "Do they, Dad?" he asked the next minute, turning his attention back to the highest authority in his life.

"Not that I know of," Clint said. "Why don't you focus on getting this job done so we can call it a day and finally get something to eat?" he suggested to his ranch hand.

Jake inclined his head as he wrapped his hands around the shaft of the sledgehammer. "Sounds good to me," he agreed.

"And me!" Ryan spoke up, his eyes shining as he added his voice to Jake's.

Clint merely nodded, applying himself to the job at hand. "Less talking, more doing," he told his crew of one and a half.

In his mind, he was already thinking himself past the next few hours, to a time when this meddlesome schoolteacher was finally back in her car and driving back to town.

Chapter Seven

She had a feeling she was going to regret this little venture come tomorrow, Wynona thought. She had used more muscles in the past couple of hours than she had in the last year. Maybe two. Teaching had never really required much from her physically.

She tightened her grip on the hammer that she had been wielding after she had retired the sledgehammer. Her hands were really beginning to ache now, even though she was doing her best not to pay any attention to them as she went on working.

There were times, Wynona had to admit, although only to herself, that she was too stubborn for her own good. But at least in this case, it had all been for a good cause.

She wouldn't have traded the way Ryan looked at her when they finally knocked off for the day for anything in the world. Up until now, she had thought that "literally beaming" was just an expression. But Ryan really *was* beaming.

"You know," Roy said to her as he leaned against the newly fixed section of fence, "they certainly didn't have teachers like you back when I was in school. If they had, I would have been really tempted to stay back in the second grade for at least an extra year—or two."

"Temptation wouldn't have had anything to

do with it. You would have been kept back because kids are brighter these days than they were back when you went to school," Clint said as he walked up behind his brother and his son's teacher.

Although he'd addressed his brother, Clint hadn't come over to engage Roy. He was looking over the work that his son's teacher had completed. The truth of it was, he was looking for shoddy work and oversights, something to point out and criticize.

Clint frowned.

There wasn't anything to find fault with. He'd had a feeling that there probably wouldn't be.

Still, he examined the work long and hard, going over it slowly.

He found nothing wrong with it. Because, at bottom, he was a fair man, Clint resigned himself to giving the woman her due.

But glowing words were not his long suit. "Not bad for a teacher," he finally pronounced.

Wynona drew the back of her wrist against her forehead, wiping away the sweat. "Not bad for anyone," she corrected with a toss of her head.

Clint started to comment that she certainly thought a lot of herself, but then he changed his mind. She was right. It *was* a good job for anyone.

After a moment he nodded. "I guess you're right," Clint agreed.

About to walk away, he noticed that Wynona was rubbing her thumbs against her fingers. She probably didn't even realize it, he thought. He was acquainted with that movement. Unlike the rest of them, the teacher hadn't worn gloves while she'd worked.

The palms of her hands had to hurt like hell, he thought.

Roy nodded toward the house. "We'd better get a move on and wash up for supper before Lucia decides that she's being ignored and makes life really hard for us," he advised, changing the subject.

Wynona looked at the younger Washburn. Roy had to be pulling her leg, she thought. She couldn't visualize the housekeeper making any sort of a fuss, much less pitting herself against Ryan's father. The man didn't strike her as someone who had a sense of humor. Moreover, she had a feeling that the milk of human kindness just curdled in his veins.

But she was the outsider here and she wasn't about to say anything that would contradict Roy in any way, so she pretended to go along with the possible "threat" he'd just voiced.

"Then I guess we'd better get moving, right, Ryan?" she asked, smiling down at the boy.

It was obvious that Ryan was surprised to

be included in the conversation. Surprised and pleased.

"Yes, ma'am," he responded quickly, "we sure better."

As Ryan shyly slipped his small hand into hers, the pain she felt surprised her. Caught off guard, Wynona winced slightly, but she made no move to break the link between them.

Her palm was throbbing. She was actually getting calluses already, she realized. How did that happen so fast?

"Something wrong, Miss Chee?" Ryan asked, concerned.

"Nope, nothing at all," she assured the boy cheerfully. "I'm just looking forward to eating Lucia's dinner."

The answer satisfied Ryan and he moved faster, leading her into the house and then the small dining area where they took meals in the evening.

Wynona saw Washburn watching her. The man was undoubtedly waiting for her next wrong move, she thought, determined not to make one.

"So, you survived," Lucia declared with an approving nod as she walked in from the kitchen carrying a tureen filled with the stew she had just finished making. "Glad to see that."

She really wanted to run some cold water over her hands, Wynona thought. They were really beginning to sting.

"Where can I wash up, please?" she asked the housekeeper.

"The bathroom is right past the kitchen," Lucia answered. Setting the tureen down, she pointed toward the passageway.

"I'll show you," Clint offered gruffly. The surprised look on Roy's face didn't go unnoticed, but Clint made no comment as he led the way to the bathroom.

"Thanks," Wynona murmured when they reached what amounted to a powder room. When Clint gave no indication that he was leaving, she told him, "I can take it from here."

Clint ignored the obvious hint. Instead, he moved her to one side. With her out of the way, he opened the medicine cabinet. Taking out a small jar from the bottom shelf, he placed it on the rim of the sink.

"Here, this might help," he told her.

"Help?" Wynona questioned. She had no idea what he was talking about.

"Yeah." Since she didn't seem to understand what he was saying, he explained further. "Rub a little into your hands, especially on your palms. It's something my mother came up with for my father. Back when he used to work the ranch, he'd come home at the end of the day and the calluses on his hands would be bleeding."

"Didn't he have any gloves?" she asked, thinking of what Washburn had said earlier to her about needing a pair of gloves.

"Kept losing them" was all he said as he left the bathroom.

"Thank you," Wynona called after Clint. His unexpected act of kindness had thrown her off for a moment.

She thought she heard Washburn grunt in response but she wasn't sure.

Gingerly opening the jar—right now even the slightest movement was beginning to really hurt—she took just the smallest bit of what looked like off-white salve on her fingertips and gingerly spread it over one palm.

It stung immediately and she sucked in her breath. The pain began to dissipate. Within a minute her calluses were only mildly sore. Encouraged, Wynona repeated the process, spreading the salve onto the calluses on her other palm.

She waited a minute just to make sure that there wasn't some delayed reaction that would cause tears to spring to her eyes, but there wasn't. What she did feel was relief.

Washburn had actually done something kind, she thought in amazement as she walked back into the dining room.

She saw Washburn watching her, a mildly curious expression on his face.

"It worked," she told him.

Immediately curious, Ryan asked, "What worked?"

She took the vacant seat next to the boy. "Your dad gave me this jar of salve to use on my calluses," she told him. "I haven't done that kind of work for a long time and I got calluses almost right away."

Ryan took his teacher's hand closest to him

and he gently turned it over to examine. He looked genuinely concerned.

"Oh." He raised his eyes to her face. "Does it hurt a lot?"

"It did," Wynona answered solemnly. "But not anymore, thanks to your dad. My hands look a lot worse than they are," she assured Ryan. She'd heard the sympathy in his voice and she didn't want him to feel bad about her hands. "Besides, a little hard work never killed anyone, right?" she asked.

"Right," Ryan echoed.

Aware that Washburn was studying her—did he expect her to complain? she wondered—she tactfully redirected attention to the dinner in the middle of the table.

"That smells wonderful," she said with enthusiasm, then looking at Ryan's father, she asked, "Can we get started?"

Rather than say anything, he merely gestured at the tureen, indicating that she take the first serving. Instead, she took Ryan's plate and dished out some of the stew onto it before taking some for herself.

It was obvious that Ryan appreciated her attention. Smiling from ear to ear he cried, "Thank you." And then he surprised her by politely waiting until she had served herself before he started to eat.

She couldn't let that pass unnoticed. Raising her eyes to Clint's, she said, "Your son has wonderful manners. You should be very proud of him."

"I am." Clint's staccato tone indicated that he didn't need her to tell him that he should be proud of his son.

Can't win for losing, Wynona thought.

The old adage ricocheted through her head and it was never truer, in her opinion, than it was right now.

Still, all in all, she had been somewhat successful this afternoon. At least she had shown Washburn that she wasn't just some helpless woman who was all talk. She'd done something to back up her words as well as pitch in. That had to mean something.

Wynona took her leave shortly after dinner was over. She said her goodbyes to the housekeeper, thanking Lucia for a delicious dinner.

Lucia took the words as her due, but then smiled warmly and squeezed her hand. "I hope to see you again."

Wynona merely smiled rather than say anything in response because whether or not she returned wasn't up to her. At least not a third time.

It came as no surprise to her that Clint had made himself scarce as she began to leave. It was Roy who walked her to her car.

"I hope you weren't too uncomfortable at dinner," he told her. "Clint's not exactly at his best when it comes to company."

Wanting to spare Roy, Wynona said, "You don't have to apologize for him."

After all, it wasn't Roy's fault that his brother was difficult, to say the least.

"I kind of feel that I do," Roy told her. When she looked at him, puzzled, he told her, "He wasn't always like this."

Wynona nodded. "So you said."

Reaching her car, she thought that would be the end of it. She opened her car door and got in. But when she went to close the door, Roy put his hand on it, stopping her.

"Is there something else?" she asked Clint's brother.

"Yeah. Ryan wanted me to give you this," Roy said, handing her something. "You'll probably need to put some more on tomorrow."

He was talking about the salve. Apparently, Clint had put some in a smaller jar for her. The thoughtful gesture doubly surprised her. Looking at the salve, she smiled. "Tell him thank you."

She waited for Roy to withdraw his hand, but he didn't. He continued to hold on to the door. "There's something else, isn't there?"

For a moment Roy looked as if he was going to say no, there wasn't, and just close her door for her. But then he apparently had a change of heart.

"Yeah, there is," he admitted.

"What is it?" she asked when he continued to wrestle with his thoughts.

Looking at her, Roy made his decision.

"Ryan's mother walked out on Clint when Ryan was less than nine months old," he told her.

Whatever she thought Roy was going to

say, it certainly wasn't this. The revelation appalled her. "She just abandoned her baby?" she cried, stunned.

Roy nodded. "Yeah. We came home after putting in one of those grueling twelve-hour days and found Ryan in his crib, howling and wet. Susan was nowhere to be found. I can still hear Clint calling her name as he went from room to room. When he picked Ryan up, that was when he saw the note. She'd left it in Ryan's crib."

Roy's face clouded over as he recalled the incident. "The note was brutally short. Susan told my brother that she didn't want to be a rancher's wife anymore. That she wasn't cut out for it, or for being a mother, either." Roy shook his head. "I'm not even sure if she said that she was sorry. What I do know is that she cut out my brother's heart with that note. I saw him change right before my eyes from the fun-loving, hardworking brother I grew up with to this hardened, angry man I barely recognized."

Recalling that day, Roy's face hardened. "Because she had hurt him so badly, Clint just separated himself from everyone. It was like he just couldn't feel anything anymore. There's no other way to say it. I know he loves Ryan," Roy said quickly, not wanting Wynona to misunderstand. "But the risk of being hurt again is just something he can't face. So he doesn't." Letting out a long breath, Roy searched her face as if to see if she understood. "I just thought you should know."

It was a lot to take in. Wynona slowly nodded her head. "Thank you. I appreciate you sharing that with me." Her eyes held his. "For your own sake, I think you shouldn't tell him that you told me. Most men don't appreciate being regarded as vulnerable by other people, especially someone they think of as an outsider."

Roy laughed softly. "You're pretty smart, you know."

She accepted the compliment while making light of it. "That's what it says on my teaching degree," she told the man.

"Ryan's a lucky kid to have you for his teacher," Roy said as he finally closed her car door for her.

"Just doing my job," she replied just before she started her vehicle.

And the rest of my job, Wynona thought as she drove away from the ranch, *is to find a way to get Clint Washburn to come back among the living.*

For both Ryan's sake and his own, she decided.

"You'll be happy to know that I didn't starve even though you didn't come home to make dinner," Shania informed her cousin playfully when Wynona walked in the door. "When you didn't show up at five, I went to Miss Joan's. She asked after you, by the way and…"

Shania's voice trailed off as she took a closer look at Wynona. There was some dirt on her cousin's clothes that she was certain hadn't been there this morning and Wynona looked worn out in general. "I told her you were fine but I think I was lying."

Her body was really starting to ache now. When she'd crossed the threshold, all Wynona wanted to do was reach the sofa.

Now that she had, she all but collapsed onto it.

"What are you talking about?" Wynona asked, shifting as she tried to find a comfortable position. There really wasn't one.

"Well, for one thing you look like someone rode you hard and put you away wet."

Shania was standing directly in front of her now, assessing her condition. "What did you do today?"

"I taught," Wynona answered. Dropping her head against the back of the sofa, she closed her eyes. Her body just continued aching.

"Taught what? Ditch digging 101? You don't get to look that exhausted just from teaching eight-year-olds."

"Eight- *and* nine-year-olds," Wynona corrected, her eyes still closed.

"Oh well, that explains it. Getting those nine-year-olds to listen is like herding cattle—" Shania replayed her words in her head. "Wait, you went out there again, didn't you?"

Wynona opened her eyes. "Went where?" she asked innocently.

"You are many things, Wyn," Shania said, exasperated, "but an actress is not one of them. Now, stop trying to throw me off the track and explain to me why you have this desire to keep beating your head against a concrete wall—because that's what you're doing, you know. Trying to reason with a man who wouldn't know reason if it bit him on the butt."

Wynona sat up, her aches and pains no longer the center of her attention, at least temporarily.

"How would you know what Clint Washburn's like?" she asked defensively.

That was simple enough to answer. "Because you're my cousin and I love you so I asked around."

Now it began to make sense.

"You talked to Miss Joan, didn't you?" The woman who ran the diner—the only restaurant in Forever—for as long as anyone in town could remember had a reputation of knowing everyone's business before they knew it themselves.

Shania shrugged. "I might have."

"Might have my foot. You went to Miss Joan's on purpose to pump her for information," Wynona stated.

"Oh please, since when does anyone have to pump that woman?" Shania asked. "She gives you her opinion whether you ask for it or not."

Wynona sighed. "And what is her opinion of Clint Washburn?" she asked. But before her cousin could answer, Wynona stopped her. "No, don't tell me. She thinks that he's a hard-hearted SOB and she doesn't like him, right?"

Instead of saying yes, Shania surprised her by saying, "Try again."

Wynona's body was really aching in earnest now and she was in no mood for guessing games. She felt her temper slipping away from her.

"Why don't you tell me, then," Wynona retorted, waiting.

"She thinks that he was given a raw deal seven years ago. Miss Joan wouldn't go into details, said that was a private matter for Clint to share when he felt up to it. But she did say that he's sealed himself off because of what happened back then." Shania paused for a beat, looking at her cousin. "Miss Joan told me to tell you to be careful."

Some things never changed no matter how much time passed, Wynona thought. Miss Joan was still dispensing advice even if she wasn't asked for it.

"She has nothing to worry about. I intend to be careful," she replied.

Shania looked at her cousin, a knowing expression on her face. "But you're not going to back off, are you, Wyn?"

"If by 'back off' you mean am I going to stop being Ryan's teacher, then no, I'm not going to 'back off,' Shania."

Shania sighed and shook her head. "That's not what I meant and you know it," she said quietly.

Chapter Eight

Rather than get drawn into an argument or become defensive, Wynona just wearily told her cousin, "Shania, I love you more than anyone else in this world, but right now I am really not in the mood to listen to any lengthy lectures."

Shania held her hands up in a mute protestation of innocence.

"No lectures," she promised.

"Okay," Wynona said, deciding to reword

her last statement. "No warnings or 'advice for my own good,'" she told her cousin.

As if on cue, Belle came trotting over to her and put her head on Wynona's lap. The German shepherd raised her soulful brown eyes up to her face.

Wynona smiled at the dog. "This is what I need right now."

Shania laughed. "I don't think there's enough room in your lap for both of our heads, Wyn, but I'll take that under advisement for the next time that I feel inclined to give you a little well-intentioned cousinly advice."

Her eyes closed, Wynona nodded in response. "That's all I ask," she replied as she began to lightly stroke their pet's head.

It amazed her how such a basically simple action could have such a calming effect on both her and the dog, she silently marveled.

Too bad Clint Washburn couldn't take lessons from the German shepherd.

The thought made her smile.

After a moment Wynona asked, "Was Miss Joan her usual self?" As she sat there, she continued to stroke Belle. She could feel the dog turning her head into her hand, trying to absorb as much of the stroking as possible.

"You mean did she ask questions?" Shania asked, not sure what her cousin was asking her.

Opening her eyes, Wynona looked at her cousin. They both knew that asking questions was what Miss Joan did. It was as much a part of the woman as the air she breathed. That and, in her own unique way, caring about the various residents of Forever.

"Yes."

Shania laughed to herself. "This is Miss Joan. What do you think?"

Wynona sat up, suddenly alert. "What did she want to know?"

Shania shrugged as she sat down beside her cousin. "The usual. How I was doing. How *you* were doing. Did we find life here disappointing after being in Houston for all those years."

Wynona interrupted her before Shania continued. "And what did you tell her?"

Shania shrugged, as if Wynona already knew the answer to that. "That it took a little bit, but we were adjusting to the change. And I told her that we both enjoyed what we were doing now."

That didn't seem like it would be enough to satisfy Miss Joan. The woman was known to dig deep when it suited her.

"And that's it?" Wynona questioned.

Shania pretended to think for a moment,

then said, "I didn't tell her about the dismembered body in your suitcase."

"Say what?" Wynona cried, stunned. Her surprise quickly faded into impatience. "I'm being serious, Shania."

Obviously, Wynona's sense of humor had taken a leave of absence. "You make it sound like there's some big secret we're trying to keep from Miss Joan," Shania said, explaining her flippant remark. "There isn't." With a sigh, she added, "I almost wish there were."

"Why?" Wynona asked, confused.

"Well, for one thing, it might make life more interesting," Shania commented.

Wynona frowned. "Life's plenty interesting just as it is," she told her cousin. She looked at Shania, trying to figure out if there was something wrong.

Shania shrugged, giving in to indifference just for a moment. "If you say so."

"Why?" Wynona asked, looking at her more closely. "You miss Houston?"

"What I miss are activities," Shania admitted. She hadn't thought she would, but she did. Maybe she was just restless, she thought, looking for an explanation. "Houston's not New York, but there were always things to do there. Here," she said, a touch of regret slipping into her voice, "not so much." She sighed. "Not unless you're into watching grass grow."

"It's not that bad," Wynona protested. She pressed her lips together. Had she missed something? "I didn't know you felt that way."

Embarrassed, Shania flashed an apologetic smile at her. "Not usually, just once in a while. I miss going out Friday nights—"

They had gotten caught up in lesson plans and schedules, but that was only because everything was still very new and needed to be worked out. Things would settle down soon.

"We could still go out Friday night," Wynona pointed out.

Shania shook her head. "It wouldn't be the same thing."

She knew what Shania was saying. "I grant you that Murphy's isn't exactly a place that people make plans to visit on their way through Texas," Wynona agreed, "but you can have a good time there. In addition, there's a comfortable feeling knowing that you're safe and that no one wants to take advantage of you."

Everything Wynona said was true, but still… "It's also not exactly earth-shatteringly exciting, either," Shania replied.

Where was this going? "So, what are you saying? You want to go back to Houston?" Wynona asked.

The thought surprised her because she thought that she and Shania were on the same page as to what they wanted to accomplish with their lives. They wanted to give back to the community where they were born. Had she pushed her own agenda on her cousin without having realized it?

Shania sighed. She realized she was being whiny. "No, I just want to complain a little, that's all," Shania admitted. "Forever's a little bit of a culture shock after life in Houston, but you're right," Shania told her. "It is a good trade-off. And I remember that you and I made that promise that one day we'd come back and do some good here. In essence that was payback for the fact that if it weren't for Great-Aunt Naomi, we might have wound up like a lot of those people who were around us while we were little girls on the reservation."

Smiling in earnest now, she turned toward Wynona. "I want to hear all about it."

"Hear about what?" Wynona asked. Shania had changed the subject and Wynona found herself lost.

Belle, meanwhile, had grudgingly moved over to make more room for her other mistress, but she didn't move far. The dog made it abundantly clear that she wanted to remain in the middle of her mistresses since most of her day was spent being alone.

"Just why did you go back to Washburn's ranch?" Shania asked her. "I thought you said that Ryan's father seemed to come around a little and he let the boy work with him."

"That's just it," Wynona answered. "I went to the ranch because I wanted to tell Washburn how happy Ryan had been in class today. He seemed totally different," she added.

"And?" Shania asked, sensing the situation wasn't as simple as that.

Wynona took a breath. "When I got there, Washburn, his brother and the ranch hand were working on mending breaks in the fence. I didn't see Ryan anywhere," she added quickly.

"And you wanted to know why," Shania guessed.

"What makes you say that?" Wynona asked.

Shania smiled. "Because I know you, Wyn," she told her cousin. "What was his excuse?" she asked. "And did you let him live?"

"Yes." She answered the last question first. "Because he didn't need an excuse. It seems that Ryan had just gone into the house to get something. Washburn had had him helping all along this afternoon."

"All right," Shania said, nodding. "If that

was the case, why didn't you just turn around and come home? You obviously stayed. Why?"

"It's complicated," Wynona said, hoping that would be enough.

It wasn't. "I'm not going anywhere," Shania told her, waiting.

Grudgingly, Wynona said, "Because I volunteered to help."

"Help with what?" Shania asked. And then, belatedly, it dawned on her. "Fixing the fence?" she asked incredulously. When Wynona nodded, she could only ask in wonder, "How did that happen?"

"Not really sure." Wynona looked down at her hands. "Now I have calluses on my hands."

Shania got up from the sofa. "I think we might have something in the medicine cabinet for that," she said, beginning to go get it.

"Don't bother," Wynona called after her.

"Washburn had some kind of homemade salve to treat that. He gave me some before I left."

"Oh?" Shania's tone clearly indicated that she was intrigued.

Wynona immediately knew what her cousin was thinking. "Don't 'oh' me. He gave it to me because he was feeling guilty about the calluses."

"This from the man who, according to you, doesn't feel anything," Shania said sarcastically.

"I got some insight into that, too," Wynona told her cousin.

Even Belle raised her head, detecting Wynona's shift in tone.

Shania grinned, her previous malaise already forgotten. "Wow, you really did have a productive visit there. What kind of insight?" Shania prodded, curious.

Wynona took a moment to reflect before answering. A great many things had changed in Forever since they had lived here ten years ago. There was a hotel in town now, as well as a law firm. Granted there were only two lawyers in the firm: the sheriff's wife, Olivia, and Miss Joan's step-grandson, Cash. But those people were new to Forever, as well, although Cash, like Shania and herself, had returned to Forever after a long absence.

The most important change in the town's dynamics, however, was the medical center. Its doors had been closed for over thirty years, ever since the last doctor had left town. It didn't reopen until Dr. Daniel Davenport came to Forever. Opening the medical center's doors had been his way of paying back his late brother. It was the latter who had initially been slated to come to Forever to practice.

Once the medical center's doors were re-opened, it slowly drew two more doctors and two nurses to the little town to join in. They had also wound up marrying residents and permanently settling down in Forever.

With such an influx of new people, it wouldn't have surprised Wynona if Miss Joan had missed ferreting out Clint Washburn's story. But she obviously hadn't. She seemed to know the story that Roy had told her in confidence. The woman had just decided that it wasn't her story to tell, beyond warning her to "be careful."

Miss Joan had her own code of ethics, Wynona mused.

Wynona could see that her cousin was waiting for her to tell her what she'd learned.

"Washburn's brother told me that Washburn came home one night to find that his wife had just taken off, leaving behind Ryan. The boy was less than a year old at the time."

"Taken off?" Shania repeated. "Taken off with whom?" she asked.

"With nobody, I gathered," Wynona answered. "Or at least if there was someone, his brother didn't mention it to me. But the upshot of it was that she didn't want to be a mother and she didn't want to be a rancher's wife. She'd left a note stating as much."

"Insult to injury," Shania commented. "That kind of thing is pretty rough on a guy's ego," she said sympathetically.

"Not to mention his heart," Wynona told her. In her estimation, egos really didn't count. It was the heart that did. "From what I gathered, after that, Washburn pretty much just kept everyone at arm's length. He still does."

"And yet he gave you salve," Shania reminded her, smiling broadly. To underscore her point, she fluttered her lashes at her cousin.

Shania was making too much out of the simple act, Wynona thought. "Washburn was just being a decent person," she insisted.

"Which tells you what?" Shania asked, temporarily treating her cousin as if she was one of her science students.

Agitated, Wynona blew out a breath. She knew what her cousin was trying to get across. "That underneath all that barbed wire he's got wrapped around himself is a decent person."

Shania smiled triumphantly.

"Bingo," she declared. "Okay," she said, regrouping. "Now that you realize that, we need to get *him* to realize that."

Shania wasn't the type to just throw words around. "You're working on an idea, aren't you?" Wynona asked, wondering if she should be bracing herself.

Shania nodded. "Washburn needs to start socializing. Right now, except for his brother and that ranch hand you said is working for him, he's practically a hermit. That's not good for him or for his son."

She already knew that part. "What do you have in mind?" Wynona asked. "Tossing a net over him and dragging him off the ranch to wherever this party of yours is being held?"

Shania hadn't thought out logistics yet. She did now. "We could throw a get-acquainted party at Murphy's," she said, referring to the town's only saloon.

Owned by three brothers, it was run by the oldest, Luke, who coincidentally was married to the town's third doctor. Rather than a bar, the saloon was more like a tavern where family members, even children, were not out of place.

"You still haven't answered how you plan to get him there," Wynona pointed out.

Shania thought for a moment. "From the way you described Washburn, a simple invitation isn't going to cut it."

"I could enlist his brother," Wynona declared.

"And if that doesn't work?" Shania asked, playing devil's advocate.

Wynona grinned. "We could always sic Miss Joan on him."

"I've got a better idea," Shania said, cutting her short.

"Okay, I'm open to suggestions," Wynona answered, waiting.

"*You* invite him," Shania said simply.

Wynona stared at her. "Me? I'm not nearly as good at persuading people to do what I want them to as Miss Joan is."

Shania gave her a knowing look. "It wasn't

Miss Joan that he gave that salve to," she reminded her cousin with a smile.

Wynona waved a hand at her, dismissing what her cousin was saying. "That doesn't mean anything."

Shania just continued looking at her. "Doesn't it? You made the man seem like a complete ogre, yet that ogre went out of his way to give you something to help ease the pain you were experiencing from the calluses you got while working on his ranch. That means something in my book."

"You do have a way of twisting things around, don't you?" Wynona asked.

"No, I can just see things more clearly than you do at times," Shania answered. "We complement each other that way," she added with amusement. "I see things you don't while you see things that I don't. It balances everything out," Shania concluded. She let her words sink in, never taking her eyes off her cousin's. "I mean, you won't *have* to try to convince him to come to this party. You can just let him continue living in that solitary prison of his, emotionally removed from his son, his brother and everyone else in the world. After all, we all know you have more than enough to do to keep busy without taking on soul-saving."

"All right, all right. If I invite the man personally, will you stop trying to bury me in your rhetoric?" she asked.

"Of course I'll stop. If you say you're going to go talk to him, then there's no need for me to go on talking, is there?"

"I should be so lucky," Wynona said with a weary laugh.

"Don't worry. I have a feeling you will be. Once you invite him," Shania added.

Wynona had no idea what her cousin was

talking about. But even so, she couldn't help thinking that she had somehow walked into a trap of her own making.

Chapter Nine

In the end, after considering all the various options open to her, Wynona decided that the best way to go about drawing Clint Washburn out and make him at least a little more social was to hold an "Open School Night." This way he couldn't accuse her of singling him out from the other parents. The focus of Open School Night would be the students with the idea of getting the parents involved with the current curriculum.

"Hey, sounds good to me," Shania said when Wynona bounced the idea off her. "I'd take it up with your principal if I were you," she encouraged Wynona.

So she did. Adele Wilson gave it her blessings. The event was scheduled in two weeks to give everyone enough time to make the necessary arrangements at school and also on the home front. It also gave the parents enough time to send back replies to the invitations.

In order to fit everyone into the small school without resorting to overcrowding, it was decided to hold the event over the course of two evenings. Grades one, two and three would come the first evening while grades four, five and six would attend on the following evening.

Wynona got her own students involved by having them make up the invitations that were going out to their parents. Even at this age, there were a couple students who showed real promise when it came to artwork. She encouraged them to help the others.

Responses started to come in almost immediately and continued arriving over the next several days. By the end of a week, everyone had acknowledged and returned the invitations.

Except for Washburn.

Well, she had known that this wasn't going to be easy, Wynona thought. She gave it another day, hoping against hope that Washburn would come around—secretly feeling that most likely, he wouldn't.

When Ryan began to slowly withdraw again, Wynona decided that it was time for her to beard the lion in his den. After school was over and she had finished preparing the lesson for the following day, she rode out to Washburn's ranch.

She spent the entire trip to the ranch giving herself a pep talk.

"You know, to some people, this might be viewed as the definition of harassment," Clint said.

He was facing away from the stable entrance when he said it.

When she had arrived at the ranch, Wynona had encountered Jake first. Looking pleased to see her, the ranch hand seemed to know why she was there. Before she could ask, he directed her toward the stable where Clint was currently working on mending some of the bridles that looked as if they were about to fall apart.

His back was to the doorway and Wynona was trying to find a way to announce herself without startling him. Washburn had caught her off guard with his statement.

Stunned, she came forward. "How did you know I was here?"

"Roy and Jake don't wear perfume," he answered matter-of-factly.

She was about to protest that neither did she, but then she caught herself. The splash of perfume she applied in the morning was so automatic—her one indulgence to femininity—that half the time she didn't even realize she was doing it.

"Very good," she murmured, feeling it best to start out by saying something positive to the rancher.

When Washburn made no response to her comment, she decided she had nothing to lose. She launched into the reason she had come to the ranch, seeking him out, this time.

"I'm here about the invitations that were sent out to the school's Open School Night."

As she spoke, she took a few more steps closer to the silent man.

Turning his head, Clint spared her a single glance, then went back to focusing his attention on the bridle he was repairing. "Figured you might be."

The man was definitely *not* a sparkling conversationalist, she thought. Taking a breath, Wynona tried again. "You didn't send it back."

"No, I didn't," he answered matter-of-factly.

The man really did require a great deal of patience, she thought, digging deep for hers. Unearthing it was not easy. "Why?" she asked.

His shrug was indifferent. "Figured not sending it would get my message across."

"What message?" Wynona pressed, hoping that it wasn't what she thought it was.

He still didn't turn around to look at her.

Instead, he continued working on the worn bridle. "That I wasn't coming."

All right, so it *was* the message she thought it was. But she wasn't about to give up. "Why not?"

This time he did turn around to look at her. There was no warmth in his eyes as he sized her up. "I don't have to explain myself to you."

"No, you don't," she surprised him by agreeing. "But since this does involve your son—and you being the only parent not attending will make him feel like an outsider," she stressed, "I thought I'd come and try to convince you to give up a couple of hours for your son's sake. It's all going to be informal and there'll be cookies," she added quickly, hoping the thought of food might be appealing to him. She was willing to try anything at this point to get Ryan's father to come around.

She should have known better.

"I'm not a kid to be bribed with treats," Clint informed her flatly.

"No, you're an adult and sometimes, as an adult you have to do things you don't feel like doing for the sake of the son you brought into the world," she told him, trying to make him see the harm his nonattendance would do. "Do you want him to feel different because he's the only one whose parent didn't attend Open School Night? Do you have any idea what that feels like when you're a kid?" she asked, passion entering her voice. "It's awful."

Putting his tools down, he faced her squarely. "Oh, and you speak from experience?" Clint asked. It was obvious that he was mocking her.

Instead of flinching, the way he'd expected, Wynona's eyes met his defiantly.

"Yes," she answered with a quiet ferocity, "I do. I know exactly what it's like to be the odd kid out, even in an area where half the kids in school only had one parent."

Clint regarded her with skepticism, but he didn't come out and ask her to elaborate.

She did anyway. To an extent.

"I lived with one parent, and let me tell you, it was hard, especially because she wasn't well." It wasn't something that she usually talked about. Her history was a private matter, even though she and Shania had gone through it together. But if it helped Washburn to understand that his actions could have unwanted consequences, then it was worth it.

He looked at her for a long moment, as if weighing whether or not to believe her. "Kids get what they need from more than their parents. It's different these days," he finally said.

"Not so different," Wynona contradicted. "Kids still look to their parents for moral support. Ryan's no different. He sees you as his first line of defense. And you should be glad of that."

Clint raised an eyebrow. "Oh?"

"Yes, you should," she insisted. "There are lots of parents who only wish they had kids who looked up to them instead of just ignoring them. Your son looks up to you and you don't appreciate it."

Clint looked at her. The impatience etched into his face was not as pronounced as it had been. But his tone wasn't exactly friendly.

"How long do you plan on standing there, yammering at me?" he asked.

Wynona didn't even hesitate. "Until you agree to come."

He believed her. He could see that he wasn't going to be able to finish his work until he gave in. "And that's all it'll take?"

"Yes," she informed him firmly.

His eyes narrowed. He was trying to discern something, she thought, but she had no idea what.

"And if I say yes," he finally said, "are you telling me that you're naive enough to think I'll actually show up?"

His expression was impassive as he spoke. Was he telling her she was a fool to just take his word? But Wynona considered herself to be a good judge of character and that was what she was banking on right now.

"I'm not naive," she told him. "You're a man whose word means something to him. So if you say you'll do something or be somewhere, then you will." She smiled at Ryan's father, confident she was right. "Tell me I'm wrong."

The words hovered on his lips and very nearly came off his tongue. But if they had, if he told her she was wrong, he'd be lying.

Because she was right.

Clint frowned at her. "What I *can* tell you is that you're a colossal pain in the neck."

"I can live with that," Wynona answered philosophically, clearly taking no offense. "So, will you come?" she asked, quickly adding, "It'll mean the world to Ryan."

Shaking his head, Clint blew out an exasperated breath. "Still don't see why."

"Because you're his hero."

Clint waved a dismissive hand at her statement. "Now you're just imagining things."

"No, I'm not. All you have to do is look into Ryan's eyes, Mr. Washburn. Your son wants to be just like you when he grows up," she told him, then challenged, "do you want him growing up to be a withdrawn, uncommunicative man?"

"So now you want me to transform for him?" Clint asked.

"No," Wynona answered honestly. "But you

might want to transform for yourself. I think that both you and your son will be happier if you do."

So now she was professing to be able to psychoanalyze him? How did she know what it took for him to be happy? Just who did this woman think she was?

"I'll be happier if you just stop preaching at me and go away," he told her bluntly.

They had circled back to what she'd already told him. "You already know how to make that happen," she reminded him cheerfully, adding, "It's just one evening, Mr. Washburn. I promise you won't regret it."

"I already regret it," he informed her. "And stop calling me Mr. Washburn," he told her. "*Mr. Washburn* was my father, who was a functioning drunk." The memory darkened his face. "My name's Clint."

Well, she was more than willing to oblige

him regarding the way she addressed him. Wynona smiled. "Nice to meet you, Clint. So, will I see you at Open School Night?" she asked again.

The woman just didn't let up. "I'm surprised you're not ordering me to be there."

Wynona shook her head. "It won't work that way, remember?" she reminded him. "You have to give me your word that you'll come to the school."

It was obvious that she was waiting for him to do just that. He had a feeling that she was also as good as her word and that she planned to stay right in front of him, talking at him for as long as it took before he cried uncle and gave in. She wasn't going anywhere until he agreed to attend this Open School Night or whatever she called it.

He blew out a long, ragged breath that was all but vibrating with weary annoyance. It really bothered him that she seemed to be able to see right through him like that. After all, the woman hardly knew him.

"All right," he bit off. "You win."

"Win what?" she asked, waiting for Clint to say the words she was waiting to hear.

His eyes narrowed. "Don't push it," Clint warned. She went on looking at him.

"Okay, you win. I'll come to Open School Night," he bit off. Clint tried not to notice that her eyes were sparkling as she looked at him.

"It's next Thursday. Seven o'clock," Wynona told him, just in case he'd forgotten.

"Yeah, I know," he snapped. "It was on the invitation."

If he thought his tone of voice intimidated her, he was wrong. Hearing his response, she looked pleased. "So you did read it."

"I had to know what I was turning down," he pointed out matter-of-factly.

"And now you don't have to," she concluded with a smile. There was no triumph in her smile, just joy. The woman was either a damn good actress, he thought, or she was genuinely verging on sainthood.

"Well, I've taken up enough of your time. I'd better leave you to your work," she said happily, backing away before he decided to change his mind.

He glared at her impatiently. "I would have been a lot happier if you'd led with that," he told her. Murmuring something under his breath, he picked up the bridle again.

"No, you wouldn't have," she answered confidently as she turned on her heel.

The remark irritated him. He didn't care for the fact that she acted like she knew things about him better than he did.

"You're awfully sure of yourself, aren't

you?" It was more of an accusation than an observation.

"Only sometimes," she told him honestly. "Only sometimes."

He watched her walk out of the stable. Clint continued to look toward the open door after she was no longer there.

The woman had managed to get to him, to burrow under his skin, creating an itch he wanted no part of. He didn't have time for it and he certainly didn't need the consequences that lay at the end if he followed that itch to its logical conclusion.

For two cents he'd just ignore the fact that he'd said he'd be at the school and just go on with his life as if nothing had happened. But something *had* happened and she was right, damn her. He wasn't the type to go back on his word after having given it, even for something as meaningless as this open school thing.

His word had been extorted from him, but he still had to keep it.

He realized that he'd almost balled up the leather strap he was trying to restore.

Damn the woman, she was undermining his thoughts. He didn't have time for this. Didn't have time to get dragged off to some meaningless session at the elementary school that his son wouldn't even remember.

Maybe he shouldn't have allowed himself to get railroaded like that.

Maybe there was still a simple way out of this if he just—

"I just saw Miss Chee," Ryan said, walking into the stable. He looked up at his father, a mixture of excitement and shyness on his face. "She said that you told her you were going to come to Open School Night." He uttered each word with an aura of hopefulness around it. "She told me that you gave her your word. Did you, Dad?"

"Why do you ask that?" Clint asked. For the first time in a long time, he found himself wondering just what was going on in that small head.

"Because I know if you really did that—if you really gave your word," he explained, "you won't go back on it. So, was she right?" he asked, allowing eagerness to enter his voice. "Did you give your word?"

He couldn't bring himself to lie and rob that look from his son's face. So he didn't. "Yeah, she's right. I did."

What happened next caught him completely by surprise. Ryan was not demonstrative. At least, he had never known the boy to be. He was quiet and obedient but not expressive.

However, this time the boy threw his arms

around his waist and hugged him for all he was worth.

Clint hardly felt the actual squeeze. After all, the eight-year-old was small for his age and Clint had had years of hard work to build up his own body so that he didn't feel things like a child's arms. But the *effect* of that squeeze, that spontaneous, gleeful hug that his son had suddenly delivered, well, that was a different matter entirely.

Like an arrow shot from a bow, his son's hug had a direct effect on the leaden part within his chest that had once been a heart.

Clint awkwardly hugged the boy back.

Chapter Ten

Wynona realized that she kept watching the classroom doorway. Given tonight's event, under regular circumstances it would have been normal to look toward the doorway every so often, especially when someone came into the classroom.

But Wynona found herself slanting glances in that direction even when there was no movement in that general area, no indication that someone new was entering the room.

There was a reason for that.

Clint Washburn wasn't here yet.

Open School Night had gotten underway almost twenty minutes ago and the rancher and his son hadn't arrived yet.

Had she misjudged the man after all? Had she placed too much faith in the sanctity of his word?

No, he was going to be here, she silently insisted. She just knew it. Washburn really believed in a code, believed in a time when a man's word actually was his bond, a bond he neither regarded lightly nor broke unless something completely unforeseeable happened.

Had it? she wondered. Had something dire happened that subsequently was responsible for keeping Washburn from accompanying his son to this event?

"Worried?"

Wynona turned around to look at her cousin. Shania had insisted on coming to Open School Night in order to lend a hand in the arrangements as well as to offer her moral support.

Right now Shania was eyeing her knowingly.

"No, it's going very well," Wynona responded, nodding around the room at the clusters of milling students. As if united in purpose, the children were almost all tugging on their parents' hands, leading them from one wall to another as they proudly pointed out their artwork from amid the rest. "Better than I'd hoped, actually," she confessed.

But Shania saw through her cousin's act and her blasé attitude. "He'll be here, Wyn," she assured Wynona in a low voice.

Wynona didn't bother to pretend that she didn't know who her cousin was talking about. A denial would have been childish and dishonest and she had never been anything but honest with her cousin. Ever.

She answered Shania in a tough tone. "He'd better if he knows what's good for him," Wynona retorted.

Shania grinned. "Ah, there's the Wynona Chee that I know and love," she declared with a laugh. The next moment her smile grew even wider. "And you are living proof that everything always comes to she who waits," Shania concluded.

Wynona stared at her cousin. "What are you talking about?"

Rather than answer, Shania merely pointed behind her, toward the doorway.

Wynona turned her head to see Ryan entering the classroom, his small fingers wound tightly around his father's hand as he led the way into the room.

Wynona hardly felt Shania's pat on her

shoulder. The next moment her cousin had made herself scarce, managing to unobtrusively meld into the gathering of parents and children. Leaving her to greet the father and son coming into the classroom.

"You came," Wynona said, addressing the remark to both Ryan and his father as she greeted them warmly.

"One of the horses got loose," Ryan said, speaking up. It was obvious that he wanted his teacher to know why they were late. "We had to get to Flora before the coyotes could find her," he explained, a very serious expression on his face.

"I understand completely," Wynona assured him. "So did you finally find her?" she asked, although she already assumed that they had because the boy didn't seem distressed.

Ryan nodded his head up and down with

vigor. "My dad's real good at finding lost animals. Horses *and* cattle," he told her proudly.

"Good thing to know in case I ever need help," Wynona said. Her eyes shifted toward the silent rancher. "Thank you for coming," she told Clint.

"Had to," he answered simply with a vague shrug of his shoulders. When she looked at him quizzically, he said, "You were holding my word hostage."

"I had nothing to do with it," she told him. "You were the one honoring your word."

Clint merely made an unintelligible sound under his breath in response. Turning his attention to the classroom in general, he asked the teacher, "So tell me, why am I here again?"

She didn't even have to pause to frame her answer. "To see firsthand how well your son is doing," she told him. Gazing down at the boy, she gently coaxed Ryan, "Tell you what.

Why don't you take your dad around and show him all your different projects?" Redirecting her attention toward the rancher, she said, "The students spent the entire day getting the classroom ready today." She smiled, oblivious to the effect her smile had on both father *and* son. "I think they're very proud of their work—and rightly so," she concluded.

Wynona could see Ryan's father looking at the various displays. The expression on his face gave her no clue what was going on in his mind so she felt obligated to add, "They all put their hearts into it."

Clint glanced at her. He had a feeling that the teacher was putting him on notice that he was to say nothing but appreciative words when talking about the work on the walls as well as the booklets that had been put together for viewing.

"Did they, now?" Clint asked, his tone giving nothing away.

Glancing around, he zeroed in on the booklet that Ryan had painstakingly put together. It was placed right below some of his artwork. Clint picked up the booklet to take a closer look.

She could see Ryan holding his breath as he watched his father leafing through the booklet.

"They certainly did," she told Clint with quiet enthusiasm that cautioned him to say only positive, glowing things about the pages he held in his hands. Moving closer to the rancher, she indicated the wall with Ryan's drawings. "I think his artwork shows a lot of promise, especially for an eight-year-old." Her eyes met Clint's. "I think your son has a great deal of talent," she said.

Clint stopped flipping through the pages

of the booklet his son had put together and looked up, his eyes meeting the teacher's.

It struck him how intensely blue her eyes were. It struck him that she could look into his very soul.

Clearing his throat, he commented, "Not much call for that kind of thing on a ranch."

Wynona glanced to see that Ryan was talking to another student. That, too, was a heartening sign as far as she was concerned. The boy was blossoming, slowly coming out of that shell he'd had around him those first few weeks of class.

Grateful that Ryan was out of earshot and hadn't heard his father's comment, she told the rancher, "Maybe Ryan won't always be on the ranch."

Clint's eyes darkened. He looked as if he was less than happy at her observation. But she felt she had to at least voice her thoughts as well as give the man something to consider.

Despite the brooding expression on Washburn's face, she pushed on. "When he grows up, he might decide he wants to do something else with his life than be a rancher. I'm not saying that he will," she quickly clarified. "I'm just saying that that door should remain open to him." Her eyes were on his again. "You do want to be fair to your son."

"Did I say that?" he questioned, as if wanting to know if he had given her that impression.

"You don't have to," she informed him. Part of her felt that she might be on shaky ground but she stood on it anyway. "You're a fair man by definition."

Clint made no response. Instead, he studied her in silence for so long, Wynona thought he had decided just to stop talking altogether.

But then he completely surprised her by saying in a grudging tone, "You're good."

For a second she thought she'd either misheard him, or imagined his response. Her eyebrows drew together as she said, "Excuse me?"

She half expected him to just walk away. But Clint didn't walk away. Instead, he explained what he was telling her. "You twist words around, saying flattering things as if they were gospel. You also make a person feel as if he was being extremely unfair if he says anything to contradict you."

He got all that from her simple answer? "I'm afraid you're giving me way too much credit, Clint," she told him, shaking her head.

Just for a moment the rancher appeared as if he was about to laugh at her. But he didn't. Instead, he responded, "If anything, I'm not giving you enough credit."

Before she had a chance to dispute his answer, Ryan had returned to his side. With a smile on his bright, shining face, the boy was eagerly tugging on his arm, wanting to bring him over to another display.

"Dad, come this way," Ryan urged. "You gotta see this one."

For a second, Clint could only stare at his son. He really couldn't get over the boy's transformation. The difference seemed almost like night and day. His son wasn't the hesitant, quiet, wide-eyed boy he'd always known up until just a few weeks ago. If anything, Ryan was like a whole new person.

The boy's withdrawn, quiet qualities had receded until they had vanished into thin air like vapors that had dried up in the fall breeze. In place of those quiet qualities were traits more in keep with the way a regular eight-year-old boy behaved.

In a way, Clint realized that he could now see himself in Ryan. Thinking back, he had been just like this when he had been Ryan's age.

Except not nearly as eager for parental approval, he recalled.

"I drew this, Dad," Ryan was proudly telling him. Then, in case his father was having trouble recognizing just what it was that he had drawn, Ryan said, "It's a picture of my horse."

"I can see that," Clint answered.

The truth of it was he was rather surprised that he actually *could* recognize what it was, given the usual nature of childish drawings.

All around them there were drawings on the walls that looked more like colorful blobs or slashes of color than anything that was actually recognizable.

Apparently, Wynona was right, Clint thought,

grudgingly giving the woman her due. Ryan did have a glimmer of talent when it came to those drawings of his. But he had to admit that he just hoped the boy had talents that lay elsewhere.

Like having a penchant for learning.

That would stand Ryan in good stead as he grew older, Clint thought.

As far as those pictures went, drawing those things wasn't going to lead to anything on its own. It certainly wasn't anything for him to consider when it came to making a living.

Clint hadn't realized that he had been looking up at the drawings for some time until he felt Ryan tugging on his sleeve.

"Do you like them, Dad?" Ryan asked. There was no missing the hope in his voice.

For a second, Clint weighed his options.

"Yes, I do," he finally answered, knowing that his response would make the boy happy.

He thought he heard a sigh of relief behind him coming from the teacher.

He had to admit, in an odd sort of way, he did like the drawing. Or rather he liked that his son could do something that he couldn't. When it came to drawing, stick figures were a challenge for him.

"I'm glad," Ryan said.

Wynona stepped back. Although she would have loved to have accompanied Clint and his son around the classroom, pointing out things and attentively listening to anything the rancher had to say about or to his son, the reality was that she had a great many more parents to talk to before the evening was over. She couldn't very well ignore them, especially after they had come out at her behest.

Slanting a last glance in Clint and Ryan's

direction, she forced herself to turn her attention toward the rest of the parents.

Wynona made herself available to answer any questions, comment on any parental observations and in general just share the evening with these parents who had come out to show their children that they supported them and were proud of them.

The evening lasted a little longer than she had initially planned, but eventually, parents began to slowly leave the classroom, their children safely in tow. Almost all of them had a few words to share with her in parting, telling her the same comment in a variety of different ways.

But in essence, what they all told her was that they appreciated that she saw as much potential in their offspring as they did. They told her, in so many words, that they were very glad that she was their children's teacher.

She had to admit that their sentiments made her feel really happy.

And then, out of the corner of her eye, she saw Clint and Ryan leaving. They were going without bothering to say anything to her. She knew she could have hung back, but given the effort she had made just to get the man to come out here, she wasn't about to just stand by and let him walk out.

Instead, she made her way over to the duo before they reached the door.

Getting in front of them, she smiled at Clint and his son.

"Thank you so much for coming," she said, taking Clint's hand and shaking it.

Rather than giving her the brush off, or mumbling, "Yeah, sure," Clint fixed her with a look. "I really didn't have a choice," he reminded her. "Did I?" He challenged her to contradict him.

Which she did.

"Actually, you did," she told him cheerfully. Before he could ask how she had come to that conclusion, she said, "You could have looked for that horse a little longer, then used that as an excuse not to attend the event tonight."

"And be accused of missing your cookies on purpose?" he asked.

There was actually humor in his voice, she thought, pleased.

"I would have set some aside and sent them home with Ryan tomorrow," she told him in the same tone that he had just used.

There was a glimmer of admiration in his eyes. "Got an answer for everything, don't you?"

"Not yet," she said honestly, "but I'm working on it."

"I'm glad we came, Dad," Ryan said, speaking up, then added, reverting back to his shy persona for just a moment, "I'm glad you came."

Taken completely aback for a moment, Clint managed to gather himself together in order to say, "Yeah, me, too." And then he looked at the woman who had all but goaded him into being here. "Me, too," he repeated, this time addressing his words to Wynona.

She smiled at him and he felt something within him responding.

He didn't want to and he didn't welcome the feeling within him, but it was there nonetheless.

Clint took a breath, steeling himself off.

With a nod of his head, he said, "Good night, Miss Chee."

Then, with his hand against his son's back,

Clint guided the boy to the door and out into the hallway.

For his part, Ryan turned around and waved at her, beaming like he had just been awarded a lifetime supply of his favorite ice cream.

And while she smiled at Ryan and returned the boy's wave, she couldn't help wondering what had just happened here. At the very last moment, Clint Washburn seemed to withdraw and take ten steps back from where they had just been only a few minutes ago.

Or was that just her imagination?

"You're frowning," Shania whispered, coming up behind her. "It didn't go well?"

"Oh, it went well," Wynona answered. "And then it didn't."

"I don't allow any riddles after seven o'clock," Shania told her. "My mind won't process them after that. Save it until morning."

Wynona was staring in the direction that Clint had taken. "I hope it's gone by morning."

"One can only hope," Shania said just before they closed up the classroom. It just seemed like the thing to say.

Chapter Eleven

There were some people living in and around Forever who considered Miss Joan to be as close to an institution as they could ask for.

Tireless, the older woman—no one really knew how old she was and no one, not even her husband, was brave enough to ask—kept the diner open seven days a week, closing only on Christmas, New Year's and Thanksgiving. On those days the people who had no family found themselves sitting at the table with Miss Joan, her husband, Harry, and anyone else who was alone on that day.

It was also generally believed that if there was anything worth knowing in the town, Miss Joan already knew about it. It wasn't that Miss Joan gossiped. She just had a way of assimilating information before anyone else even knew there was information to be gathered.

When Wynona finally decided to come into the diner to ask Miss Joan what light she could shed on Clint Washburn's self-imposed isolation, she felt rather uncomfortable about it.

She hadn't seen the woman since she had left Forever all those years ago. More important, she hadn't dropped by since she had returned. That made turning up now to ask questions particularly awkward.

As she entered the diner, Wynona tried to

think of the best way to approach Miss Joan. Arriving at the diner when she felt fairly certain that it wouldn't be full, Wynona practically tiptoed up to the counter.

The redheaded woman had her back to the door and was, from the looks of it, slicing up the freshly baked peach pie that was sitting on the counter right in front of her.

Wynona pressed her lips together, still searching for the best way to initiate the conversation.

"So are you going to just stand there admiring my hair, or are you actually going to say something, Wynona?" the woman asked, her back still to her.

Wynona's mouth dropped open. It had gone suddenly dry and she was totally speechless as she continued to stare at the woman's back.

The sound of her own breathing seemed to echo in her ears.

Finally, she found her tongue. "How did you know it was me?"

Miss Joan slowly turned around to look at her. Wynona continued to stare. It was as if the woman had some how been preserved in time. She hadn't aged in ten years.

"I'm Miss Joan. I know everything," the older woman replied simply. And then she added matter-of-factly, "And I saw your reflection in the metal cabinet."

"Oh, thank goodness," Wynona replied with a relieved laugh. "For a second I thought you actually had eyes in the back of your head."

Hazel-green eyes traveled up and down the length of her body slowly, taking complete measure of the young woman before her.

"I never said I didn't," Miss Joan replied quietly.

Finished with the pie, Miss Joan retired the long, thin knife she'd been using, letting it slide back down into the pitcher filled with hot water. She had been dipping the knife into the hot water in between cuts to ensure the pie was cut in clean, even pieces.

"You filled out some since I last saw you," she observed.

Given that her last clear memory of the woman was just before she and Shania had been taken to Houston to grow up there, Wynona could only smile. "Well, it's been more than ten years," she replied, even though she knew that Miss Joan was aware of that fact.

Miss Joan nodded her head, as if silently agreeing with Wynona's response.

"It took you this long to say hello?" the woman asked.

Wynona flushed. "Sorry," she apologized, at a loss as to how to excuse the fact that she hadn't come by even once since she'd returned to Forever. She'd been busy at first and then, the more time that went by, the more awkward just dropping by became.

Until she had a reason.

"Don't be sorry," Miss Joan told her. "Just don't let another ten years go by between visits." She looked at the elementary school teacher knowingly. "I take it you didn't drop by to see if my hair was still as red as you re-member." The laugh was dismissive. "Your cousin could have told you that."

Well, nothing had changed. The woman never did stand on polite ceremony or beat around the bush, Wynona thought. Taking a breath, she launched into the reason she had finally dropped by.

"I came to ask you what you know about Clint Washburn," she said honestly.

"Runs a ranch with his brother that their father left them before he could drink it out from under them," she said, reciting the information as if she was talking about the number of eggs that were still in her refrigerator after breakfast had finished being served. Her eyes looked into Wynona's. "You want to know about the wife, don't you?" Miss Joan said.

There was no point in pretending the question surprised her. "Whatever you can tell me," Wynona replied honestly.

Miss Joan took a cup out from beneath the counter and placed it in front of Wynona. Reaching for the coffeepot, she poured the dark brew into the cup. Done, she placed a coffee creamer next to the cup, along with a couple of packets of sugar.

"She ran off, leaving him to raise their son. Kid was little more than an infant at the time. Nine months, if I remember correctly." She shook her head. "Never knew what Clint thought he saw in that woman." She laughed shortly; there was no humor in it. "I guess the poor guy was just looking to have a family of his own." She pressed her lips together, shaking her head again. "Couldn't see past her face, otherwise he would have been able to see how empty she was."

"Empty?" Wynona repeated, trying to understand what Miss Joan was saying.

"The woman had no character," the older woman explained. "No values. Susan's world revolved around just herself, nobody else. The girl thought she was too good to live here. She wanted something else out of life than just being a rancher's wife. Or a mother," Miss Joan added.

Anger furrowed her brow and Wynona could see that it was directed toward Clint's absent ex-wife.

"Clint's a smart man but he never saw it coming." Very thin shoulders rose and fell helplessly. "Guess some people just don't see what they don't want to."

Wynona only had one more question to ask. "Does he know where she is?"

"Nobody does." Miss Joan's voice all but shouted, "Good riddance."

"Last anyone heard," she continued, "Susan was on her way out to California. I have no idea if she ever got there." Miss Joan paused, a fisted hand on her hip as she looked at Wynona. "Why aren't you asking him these questions?"

"I'm just trying to satisfy my curiosity," Wynona answered. "As for Clint, he already thinks that I stuck my nose where it didn't belong when I managed to get him to come to Open School Night for Ryan's sake."

Listening, Miss Joan nodded her head in approval. "Gotta say that's pretty impressive, Wynona, getting Clint to do that. That man isn't the kind to be browbeaten or give in if he doesn't want to." She paused, appearing to size Wynona up. Wynona did her best to meet the woman's gaze head-on and not squirm. "Anything else you want to know?"

"No, not right now," Wynona told her. "But if I do," she added with a smile, "I know who to come to."

Miss Joan accepted the response. "Okay, then. And next time," she cautioned by way of a footnote, "don't be such a stranger. I remember you when you couldn't see over the counter."

That was the woman's way of reminding her that they had history, Wynona thought. "I can see over it now," Wynona replied cheerfully.

"All the more reason to come by," Miss Joan told her before she turned her attention to tend to another customer.

Wynona opened her purse, about to leave

money on the counter to pay for her half-finished coffee.

As if sensing what she was doing, Miss Joan turned her head and gave her a sharp look over her shoulder.

"Did I say anything about paying?" she asked the younger woman.

"No, but—"

"Then put that away," the older woman ordered. With that, she went back to the other customer.

It was nice to know that there were some things that just didn't change, Wynona thought as she left the diner.

Once outside the diner, she went to her car. Miss Joan hadn't told her anything that she didn't already know, thanks to Clint's brother. What she had decided to ascertain was that there wasn't anything else that had been omitted, like Clint trying to track his ex-wife down and bring her back.

If he *had* made the attempt to do that, Wynona was certain that Miss Joan would have known. It never occurred to Wynona to question that belief.

Or to question the information the woman gave her.

The confirmation of the information just succeeded in making Wynona more determined than ever to make sure that Clint became the father that Ryan needed.

What today also did was make her determined to make Clint come around and rejoin the land of the living. As far as she was concerned, Clint Washburn had been in solitary confinement much too long. Granted that his imprisonment had been of his own making, but that didn't change the fact that he needed to wake up. Not just for his son's sake, but for his own, as well.

Wynona set her mouth, making a decision. Clint Washburn had just become her newest project.

Clint was not so withdrawn from the immediate world that he didn't notice it. Notice that his son was becoming and acting more like a real boy with each day that passed. The evidence was blatant in everything he did.

When he came home from school, Ryan talked now. Talked about his day, about what had happened at school. He talked about the kids he interacted with in class. Nothing went unsaid.

It slowly dawned on Clint that his son sounded as if he actually had friends, other children whom he talked to and seemed to be getting along with.

Clint pretended it made no difference to him, but it did and eventually, he stopped pretending because the reality was he wasn't fooling himself.

He *liked* the fact that his once quiet, withdrawn son had friends.

Having Ryan chattering to him, to Roy, to Jake and to Lucia a good deal of the time—while he did chores, while at the table and just about anytime in between—was a little more difficult for him to finally wrap his head around and get used to, but he was getting there. Faster than he'd thought.

However, the part he found the hardest for him to get used to was when the boy talked about his teacher, the woman who had had such an effect on him and had, quite literally, changed the course of his life.

"And she has a dog," Ryan was saying this particular evening at the dinner table as he once again sang the praises of his teacher. He turned to look at his father. "Did you know she had a dog, Dad?"

Suddenly realizing that his son was waiting for an answer, Clint said, "No, I didn't know that."

"Well, she does," Ryan confided, launching into a further narrative. "It's a girl dog. Her name is Belle. And she's smart and pretty, like Miss Chee. Except she doesn't have fur," Ryan specified. "Miss Chee, not the dog," Ryan said quickly in case his father wasn't following him. "And she does tricks. Belle, not Miss Chee," he felt duty bound to distinguish.

"Did Miss Chee tell you the dog does tricks?" Roy asked, interjecting his two cents into the conversation.

"No, I saw Belle doing tricks," Ryan answered with excitement. "The whole class did.

Miss Chee brought Belle to class today so we could all meet her." And just like that, he rerouted his conversation. "Can we get a dog, Dad?" he asked, looking at his father with the same hopeful eyes he'd turned on him when he'd asked his father to attend Open School Night.

"We've got horses and cattle," Clint said with a note of finality, as if that simple fact should be enough for his son.

But it was obvious that Ryan definitely had other ideas.

"And a dog could help us," Ryan told him. "If we got a dog like the one Miss Chee has, he could help herd the cattle. Maybe even the horses, too," the boy added.

He never took his eyes away from his father's face, as if confident that he could stare him down and make his father relent.

Clint wanted to say no. He had neither the

time nor the inclination to add a dog to his household.

But the look on his son's face made the word *no* just impossible to utter, no matter how much Clint wanted to.

What the hell had that teacher done to him? Clint silently demanded. How had the woman managed to turn everything upside down and short-circuit his world in such a short space of time?

He wasn't himself.

Clint frowned. He needed to have it out with Wynona Chee. Needed to tell her to stop putting ideas into his son's head. She needed to stick to educating her students and not finding ways to try to rearrange their lives the way she was obviously attempting to do with Ryan's.

Without warning, Ryan's high-pitched voice

pierced through the thoughts that were building up in his head.

"Could we have her out here for dinner again, Dad?" his son asked out of the blue, managing to completely surprise him.

"Yeah, can we, Dad?" Roy asked, unable to hide his grin as he added his voice to his nephew's.

The rather knowing expression on Roy's face got under his skin.

In response, Clint gave his brother a look that silently ordered him to knock it off. But apparently, the message was not being received because Roy just went on grinning at him as he said, "I think it's a good idea."

"You want to see the woman," Clint snapped, "do it on your own time."

Out of the corner of his eye, he saw Ryan's face fall. The boy looked crushed. This time, when his son asked, the enthusiasm had left his voice. Instead, it was replaced with a serious, somewhat sorrowful note.

"Can't we have her here so that all three of us can see her, Dad?" he asked, never taking his eyes off his father's face.

And then Lucia added her voice to the conversation. "I could make her stew," the housekeeper volunteered. "She liked it the last time she was here."

"The *only* time she was here," Clint reminded the woman.

The words seemed to have no effect on his housekeeper. They certainly weren't registering with her, he thought darkly.

Neither were they registering with his brother or, more important, with his son. Clint felt like the ground under his feet was quickly turning into quicksand and despite all of his best efforts, he found himself sinking fast.

"I'll think about it, okay?" he finally said

to his son, thinking that would be the end of it, at least for a while.

"Okay." Ryan paused for a moment, then in all innocence asked, "When will you be finished thinking about it so you can say yes?"

Roy laughed, tickled at the boy's response. "He's got you there."

When had all this happened? Clint wondered. A few months ago if he said no to something, whether to his son, his brother or the other two people at the ranch, it remained no. There were no attempts to get him to change his mind or reconsider. Certainly no hope of getting him to actually say yes to something like having a woman sit down at their table who wasn't Lucia.

How had things changed so quickly?

"Maybe she's too busy to come to dinner," Clint finally said to his son. "Remember, she's got a lot of students."

Ryan had an answer for that, too. "She told the class she'd never be too busy for us."

If his intention was to play fair, then he knew he was losing, Clint thought. Moreover, he had the feeling that Ryan would only keep after him until he finally agreed to this fool notion.

He was never going to have any peace until then.

"I can ask her for you," Ryan volunteered. "Tomorrow, before class, I can—"

"If anyone is going to ask your Miss Chee to come to dinner, it'll be me," Clint said. He meant that to terminate the discussion.

Instead, it elicited a wide smile and a happy squeal. "Thanks, Dad!" Ryan cried.

Clint opened his mouth to protest that there was nothing to thank him for, but then he shut it again. He recalled something that Wynona had said to him. She'd said that Ryan saw him as his hero, or words to that effect. For now he decided to just bask in that light.

Maybe tomorrow he'd think of a reason not to invite the teacher to his table.

Chapter Twelve

Clint gave in. This invitation to the teacher seemed to mean a great deal to Ryan. And even if the boy didn't say anything, he knew that both his brother and the housekeeper would.

It wasn't a battle worth fighting.

Clint made up his mind. If he was going to extend the invitation to the teacher to have dinner at his ranch, he was not about to do it by phone. Though in the long run it was easier that way, it was, in his estimation, the coward's way out.

And having Ryan invite his teacher the way the boy had eagerly volunteered to do somehow just didn't seem right, either. It seemed to supersede his authority. So Clint went back to his initial conclusion on the matter. The invitation needed to come from him, verbally, on a face-to-face basis.

Even so, Clint found himself coming up with spur-of-the-moment reasons not to go see her. But he could see his son becoming more antsy with each passing day. He knew it would only be a matter of time before the boy jumped the gun and did the asking himself, so finally, on Wednesday afternoon, Clint got behind the wheel of his truck and pointed the vehicle toward town.

"Hey," Roy called, coming up to the driver's side. "If you're going into town for something, I can go in your place." Unlike him, his brother looked for any excuse to drive into Forever.

"No," Clint answered, setting his jaw hard, "you can't."

And he drove away, terminating the discussion.

He'd come close, Clint thought, to handing over what he viewed as his "task" to his brother.

Even now, as he got closer to town, he couldn't believe that he was actually willingly doing this.

"It's just a dinner for the boy's sake," he muttered to himself. "That's all."

Under no circumstances could this be viewed as a date, he thought angrily. He'd sworn that he would never put himself into that sort of a situation again, a situation that allowed a woman the power to crush him into the ground the way Susan had ultimately wound up doing to him.

Besides, Clint reminded himself, he and the teacher weren't going to be alone at dinner. There was going to be a full house present. Ryan, Roy, his other ranch hand, Jake, and even Lucia would be there with them. Lucia might be making the dinner but he was going to insist that she sit down at the table with them. The more people there, the better.

No one in their right mind could possibly think of this as a "date."

He realized he was grinding his teeth and consciously made an effort to stop.

The refrain that this was *not a date* was still going through his head like a steady drumbeat when he pulled into Forever.

There seemed to be more people in town than usual, especially on a weekday. He scanned the area. A lot more, he observed.

Rather than giving the impression that they were all about personal errands, he saw people gathering together, conferring intensely.

Something was up and Clint idly wondered what it was. Was there something he should be aware of? The sky looked too clear for there to be a storm coming.

Then what?

Reaching his destination, he parked his truck in front of the elementary school and got out. He stopped the first person who crossed his path, a man he vaguely recognized as being one of the people who worked in the general store.

If it hadn't been for the charged electricity in the air, Clint might have just ignored what was going on. But something seemed to be happening and he found he couldn't turn his back on it.

That had been Wynona's work.

The man he recognized from the general store had a bunch of flyers in his hands. Clint deliberately stopped him and asked, "What's going on?"

The man, Jason Rivers, looked at him as if he thought Clint had been living under a rock.

"Haven't you heard?" he asked with a look of disbelief on his craggy face. "Tyler Hale is missing."

The name meant nothing to Clint. But before he could ask Jason who Tyler was, the man pushed one of the flyers into his hands.

"We're putting together search parties to look for him." Jason paused only long enough to tap the page before moving on. "He's been gone since yesterday."

Clint scanned the page to fill in the rest of the information.

The boy, who was the same age as his son, seemed to have disappeared on his way home from school. The photo and description nudged forward no memories for him as he committed the former to memory.

Still holding the flyer in his hand, Clint walked into the school. He just wanted to get the invitation over with.

When he found Wynona, she was just leaving her classroom. Moving quickly, he got in front of her. She didn't look surprised to see him, which gave him pause until she said, "You've come to join the search."

The amount of relief and welcoming in her voice caught him totally off guard. For a second Clint didn't know how to respond. Saying no seemed rather heartless under the circumstances, but just saying yes was nothing short of a lie and he didn't believe in lying.

Torn, he fell back on what was, at best, a vaguely worded truth. "I just heard that the boy was missing."

Wynona took his answer in stride, thinking he was explaining why he hadn't been here sooner.

"Horrible, isn't it?" she asked as she walked out of the room. "His poor parents must be out of their minds with worry."

"People handle crises in different ways," Clint told her.

"True," she agreed, then said, "The way I handle it is I just have to do something about it."

He laughed softly. She really was a scrapper. There were worse things, he supposed. "I kind of figured that."

She didn't bother trying to figure out what Ryan's father meant by that. Instead, she just took charge of the situation. She did it without thinking.

"Why don't you come with me?" she suggested. "I'm not too bad when it comes to tracking." She'd had a friend, Tommy, on the reservation when she lived there and Tommy had taken delight in passing on what seemed to come naturally to him. He had taught her how to track. "And you're probably better."

Clint had no idea why she would think that. He'd never said anything to anyone about his abilities to follow a trail that was practically nonexistent. But it sounded as if there very well might be a life at stake. Making up his mind, he didn't bother with denials or refusals.

"Let's go." His response was the only testimony to the fact that he was willing to put his skills to work.

Sheriff Rick Santiago was in charge of the search parties. There was no shortage of volunteers. He didn't think that there would be.

The residents of Forever could be counted on to look after their own.

Because the territory outside the town was vast, the sheriff divided the searchers into parties of twos and threes, and in a few cases, fours. His thinking was to use those who were inexperienced, putting them together with the more experienced trackers.

Despite the number of volunteers, there was still a great deal of area to cover.

"We'll meet back here in town right after sundown. It'll be too dark to continue the search then and I don't want to have extra people to look for." There was no humor attached to his words. "Hopefully by then one of us will have found Tyler."

Everyone got started, spreading out and calling Tyler's name. They also talked to one another in an effort to keep their spirits up as well as remain positive about the search's ultimate outcome.

Clint wasn't interested in uplifting spirits. He was focused on getting information that might help bring this search to a close faster.

"This kid ever run away before?" he asked Wynona matter-of-factly as they methodically conducted their search.

She spared him a look. "He didn't run away," she answered.

"How do you know that?" Clint challenged. He wasn't trying to be argumentative. In his mind, hunters needed to know their quarries.

"Because he's in my class," she informed him, a slight edge entering her voice. It was hard to tamp down her own concern. "He's a happy kid and his parents love him," she added as they made their way across terrain that was, for the most part, relatively flat.

There was a mountain range located in the

distance. It was covered with trees and was the area where the town's annual Christmas tree came from. But the idea of Christmas seemed a million miles away.

"You never know what's going on in someone's home," Clint answered, looking straight ahead. "Families have secrets."

She looked at him again. "I'm well aware of that," she replied.

In his own way, he was trying to prepare her for the eventuality that they might never find the boy. "Maybe something happened and this kid—"

"Tyler," she interjected, not wanting the boy to be reduced to just a dehumanized, antiseptic term. "His name is Tyler."

"Tyler," Clint obliged as he continued to lead the way. "Tyler decided to run away. Maybe to teach his parents a lesson, maybe to just get away from them, or maybe—"

"Or maybe he just had a yen, went exploring and got lost. Boys do that," Wynona insisted with feeling.

He caught the inflection in her voice. "You believe that."

"Yes," Wynona said with such passion that he could only look at her for a long moment, almost won over by her spirit.

But his practical side resurfaced almost immediately. "Well, if that's the case, if he just 'went exploring,' why isn't he back?"

Wynona lifted her shoulders in a helpless shrug. She didn't have a definitive answer to give Clint and it frustrated her.

"He got lost, he tripped and got hurt," she said, enumerating all the different things that could have happened. "He wasn't looking where he was going and fell into a hole. Or maybe he somehow got trapped."

The last word caught Clint's attention. "Trapped?" he asked.

Desperate, Wynona was still fabricating

excuses as fast as she could think of them. "A coyote crossed his path. Tyler started to cower, then he looks for someplace to hide."

Clint turned the suggestions over in his mind, reviewing them as quickly as Wynona was coming up with them. And then finally, he nodded, agreeing. "That might be a possibility."

"Thank you," Wynona replied in what sounded like a distant, emotionless voice.

Clint just assumed she was being sarcastic, but when he looked at Wynona's face, he realized that she wasn't. She was serious.

With a sigh, he signaled for her to follow him. They had a lot of territory to cover before sundown.

"We should be heading back," he told her, breaking the silence that had gone on for over the last fifteen minutes. Possibly even longer.

He gestured at the sky. The sun was setting. "It's going to be dark soon."

She knew that and she was trying not to think about it or to allow panic to slither into her mind and slow her down.

"Just a little longer," Wynona urged. "Tyler's already been out here one night and he must really be scared by now. We need to find him," she emphasized.

So far, all the signs they thought they had picked up had led nowhere, or had faded away without yielding any results. There'd been no signal from any of the other searchers that they had found the missing boy, either. It felt as if they were no closer to locating Tyler now than when they started out.

"Aren't you afraid we'll get lost in the dark?" Clint asked her.

He was curious to hear her answer. As far as he was concerned, he could still find his way back, so being out here at this point presented no danger.

"Honestly, I'm more afraid that he's lost," she answered. She scanned the area, but it was getting harder and harder to make things out. "Are there any caves around here?" she asked.

"No." And then Clint rethought his answer. "But there're a couple of large burrows."

"Where?" Wynona pressed, her excitement mounting for the first time in hours.

Something was always in the last place a person looked, she told herself. It was corny, but true. She glanced at Clint, waiting for him to answer her.

"It's been a while since I've been out around here," he told her.

She didn't want excuses; she wanted results. She could almost *feel* the boy's fear.

"Try," she stressed.

He looked at her. There was a full moon out, which helped to illuminate the area—and her. Moonlight became her, he caught himself thinking before he pushed the thought away.

Knowing that she had to have noticed him looking at her, he diverted her back to their lost boy. "You think he might be there?"

It made sense to her. "A burrow isn't very big, but neither is he. And it might be where he's hiding from the animals—and the cold. The temperature dropped when the sun went down," she reminded him. It worried her to think of the boy out here all night, cold and hungry.

Clint stood there for a long moment, scrutinizing the already progressively darker terrain. He was trying to remember the location of one of the burrows.

And then he pointed west. "I think there's a burrow over that way."

They began walking, picking up their pace. Once again Wynona began to call out the boy's name the way she had earlier. Her throat felt a bit raw but she forced herself to continue. This wasn't the time to think of her own comfort.

Nothing but night sounds answered her. There wasn't anything remotely human in that mix. Tyler wasn't responding.

Frustrated, she turned toward Clint. "You said that there were a couple of burrows out here. Where's the other one?"

As far as he was concerned, this was a losing battle and they had stayed out a lot longer than they had initially agreed to. The sheriff might even be concerned about them by now.

"You ever give up, lady?" he asked her.

"Hasn't been known to happen yet," she told him crisply.

Clint sighed. Gesturing her onward, he muttered, "Let's go."

They searched for the second burrow. Finally finding it, Wynona began calling Tyler's name yet again. There was no answer.

"C'mon," Clint urged, taking her arm. "He's not here."

She pulled her arm away. "We don't know that yet. You can go back if you want to," she said, continuing to call Tyler's name.

Clint murmured a few choice words under his breath, but he stayed at her side. He joined his voice to hers, calling out to Tyler.

Several more minutes passed. And then a weak voice, more like a sob, was heard in the distance.

"Here. I'm here. Here!" The voice grew in strength, like a last-ditch attempt before total despair set in, silencing the boy.

Instantly alert, Wynona began running toward what appeared to be another side of the burrow. She quickly cut the remaining distance down to nothing.

Clint was right beside her, his long legs eventually outdistancing her.

This part of the burrow was more like a hole in the ground that had all but caved in on itself, obscuring the opening from being seen by the casual eye.

Wynona was on her knees, calling down into the opening. "Tyler, are you in there?"

"I'm here, I'm here," the little boy cried. "I was looking for leprechauns. I thought I saw one and tried to follow, but then everything started coming down on me and I couldn't get out."

Clint was already digging, using his bare hands to get to the boy. Luckily, the dirt was soft.

Without a word to him, Wynona joined in,

trying to dig the boy out, hoping their combined effort would enable them to get to Tyler faster.

"We're coming, Tyler," she called, doing her best to keep his spirits up. "Ryan's father and I are going to get you out of there. I promise."

Clint had realized something. "Hold still, Tyler," he ordered, for once trying to keep his voice gentle instead of stern. "The dirt's soft, but if you start moving around, you might make it shift on you."

He was phrasing it euphemistically not to frighten the boy. What he was really afraid of was that the remaining dirt would cave in on Tyler, burying the boy further. They had no tools to use in order to dig him out any quicker than they were doing.

"I'm scared," Tyler cried.

"Don't be scared," Wynona told the boy. She was worried that he might panic and that would just make matters worse. "We'll have you out in a few minutes, I promise. Just hold very still. Like a statue. Can you do that for me, Tyler? Can you pretend to be a statue?"

"Like the one you showed us in that picture?" he asked, his voice trembling.

"Yes, exactly like that," she encouraged.

"Okay, I can do that," he answered, but his voice was quaking.

Clint picked up his pace even though his arms were beginning to ache and it felt like his fingers were cramping up.

"You're doing great, Tyler," he encouraged. "Just hang in a little longer, cowboy. Just a few more minutes. And then you're going to have some story to tell your friends."

"I will?" he cried, desperately trying to remain brave.

"You bet," Clint told him. "All the other kids are going to be real jealous of you." More dirt flew to the side. His shoulders were aching. "Almost there, Tyler. Almost there."

The sound of his voice seemed to calm the boy down.

Chapter Thirteen

Painfully aware that this piece of nondescript clump of earth could have easily become Tyler's final resting place if they hadn't found him, after they carefully eased the boy out of the mound of crumbling dirt, Clint rose to his feet holding Tyler in his arms.

His first thought was to head back the way they had come. But he didn't know if Wynona was up to it after what they had just gone through to rescue the boy. By all rights she should have been exhausted by now, but he couldn't very well leave her behind.

"Can you make it back to town?" Clint asked, looking at the woman next to him. She had dirt in her hair as well as smudges on her face and clothes. He knew he didn't have any other options open to him. If she was too exhausted to undertake the journey, they'd have to wait here until morning.

Though he didn't want to, he made the proposal to her. "We can stay here and rest until morning if you feel that—"

But Wynona waved away his concern. "Don't worry about me," she told him. There was no way she wasn't going to make it back tonight, even if she had to crawl. "There's no signal out here," she said, reminding him that they couldn't call anyone. "Tyler's mom and dad need to know that he's safe." She smiled at the boy. "And I think that Tyler needs to get some dry clothes on him and some warm food *into* him, don't you, Tyler?" she asked the boy.

"Yes, ma'am," Tyler answered solemnly.

Polite even in dire circumstances, someone had raised this boy right, Wynona thought.

Clint nodded. "Then if you think you're up to walking," he told Wynona, "we'd better get started getting back."

Even as he said the words, he could feel Tyler clinging to him as if he was never going to let go. The boy had really been scared, he thought. "Hang in there, Tyler," he told the boy in his arms, "we're going to get you home."

They started walking back.

Both Clint and Wynona were prepared to walk all the way back to where they had first left their car, fairly certain that by now, given the hour, the other searchers had returned to town. So when a beam of light slashed through the darkness when they were a little more than halfway back, Clint stiffened. His mind immediately braced for the worst.

"Get behind me," he ordered Wynona.

She stubbornly disregarded the instruction and instead, picked up her pace so that she was in front of Clint and the boy he was carrying.

"Damn it, woman, listen to me!" Clint ordered.

The next moment the identity of the person wielding the flashlight and shining it at them was no longer a mystery.

Sheriff Santiago lowered the small, intense flashlight he was using. The grin on his face was almost as bright.

"Boy, am I damn happy to see you!" the sheriff declared. "All three of you," he added, smiling at Tyler. He ruffled the boy's hair. Tyler continued clinging to Clint. "You gave us quite a scare, Ty," the sheriff told the boy.

"I kinda scared me, too," Tyler admitted, his voice partially muffled against Clint's shoulder.

Nodding, the sheriff pulled out the walkie-talkie attached to his belt, pressing the button on the side. "We found them," he told the deputy on the other end. "The boy as well as Washburn and the teacher."

"We weren't lost," Wynona protested.

Santiago's eyes swept over the trio. "My mistake. We thought you were," he explained. He regarded them again. "You up to walking?" he asked.

"Just don't get in our way," Wynona told him.

The sheriff laughed, then gestured them on. "Then let's go."

They resumed walking back to the initial starting point, but this time, the journey was far from silent.

"A lot of people are going to be really glad to see you," the sheriff told Tyler.

Rather than look happy, the boy hung his head. "I'm sorry I caused so much trouble."

"Never mind that now. We found you and that's what matters," Clint told him.

Tyler hung on to him even harder.

Wynona saw Clint tighten his arms around the boy. She smiled to herself despite everything that they had gone through.

The man had a heart after all.

Alerted by the deputy, Tyler's parents were waiting for him before they had a chance to broach the perimeter of the town.

Donna Hale was sobbing as she embraced her son even while he was still in Clint's arms.

"I don't know how to thank you," Ed Hale told Clint and Wynona, his voice almost breaking as he choked back his own tears.

"No thanks necessary," Clint answered. Gratitude made him uncomfortable. He turned his small burden over to Tyler's father.

It took a moment for Tyler to release his hold on Clint. Before going to his father, the boy looked at the man who had helped to dig him out, his wide brown eyes saying everything that he was unable to convey to him in words.

Clint nodded in response, then took a step back as everyone who had come out to search for Tyler closed ranks, surrounding Donna and Ed Hale and their son.

"You did good."

The simple, three-word sentence of praise came from Miss Joan, who along with some of her waitresses, had set up a station with hot coffee and pastries in the town square for those searchers who had temporarily come back to town to refuel before setting out again. It was clear that no one felt right about calling it a day and going home until the boy was found.

And now they remained for another reason. Although Tyler had been found and returned to his parents, there was still a lot of wired energy ricocheting among the residents, needing a harmless way to be rechanneled and discharged.

"Celebration's on me," Miss Joan announced, raising her whiskey voice so that everyone could hear, "now that there's something to celebrate. C'mon." She gestured for everyone in the square to follow her to the diner. There was no question in her mind that they would.

As people began to leave the square and

walk toward the diner, Wynona noticed Clint turning away.

He was going home, she thought. Moving fast, she stepped in front of him, blocking his path.

Clint raised one expressive brow. "You're in my way."

She didn't move. "Earlier today, before we started looking for Tyler, you came into the school. I got the impression you were looking for me and wanted to talk. Did you?"

All that seemed like a million years ago now, Clint thought. Wynona was looking at him, waiting for him to give her an answer.

He shrugged. "Yeah, I did."

"About?" she asked, waiting.

He knew he couldn't just walk away without answering. For one thing, the woman would follow him. He was beginning to learn that she was as stubborn as they came. So he told her.

"Ryan wanted me to ask you to come to dinner at the ranch."

"Ryan wanted," Wynona repeated. She continued watching him, as if she was waiting for more.

"Yeah."

She waited a beat, but Washburn didn't say anything further. What did she expect?

Because he had been the reluctant hero today, she cut him some slack. "And what did *you* want?"

Clint shrugged. He didn't want to be put on the spot but he didn't see a way out. Between clenched teeth, he said, "To make the boy happy."

"Then I guess I can't disappoint him—and indirectly—you," she added, taking great pains to word her response carefully.

He shrugged, as if all this was a moot point. "It's a little late for dinner now," he told her.

"But not too late for a rain check," Wynona pointed out.

He frowned. "You never not have an answer for everything?" he asked, irritated that he couldn't just walk away from all this.

Wynona smiled, the teacher in her coming out. "That's a double negative, Clint."

He blew out a breath. "Yeah, well, I guess I'm kinda tired."

"Hey, you two, Miss Joan wants to know what's taking you so long," Angel Rodriquez, the diner's resident chef, asked. "And she said to tell you not to even *think* about begging off. You two are the official heroes of this thing, finding Tyler the way you did." The woman smiled understandingly at them. She knew that Miss Joan was a force to be reckoned with, same as they did. "This celebration's as much for you as it is for him."

Wynona could feel the man next to her

bristling. She could guess what was going through his mind.

"If I remember my facts correctly," she told him, "nobody's ever crossed Miss Joan and lived to tell about it."

Clint considered saying that he would be the first, but then decided against it. After all, this afternoon he'd come to ask Wynona to come to the ranch for dinner, so in a way, the location of the meal had just been changed.

He shrugged, as if he was giving in. "Then I guess I'd better not."

"Smart man," Wynona told him with a wide smile.

They fell into step behind Angel and began walking to the diner.

"You know, you surprised me," Wynona confided to Clint in a whisper just before they reached their destination.

He was tempted to just let her remark go,

but something goaded him to take this a step further. He supposed that his curiosity had gotten the better of him.

"How?" he asked.

She smiled at him. "You went on looking when I asked you to even though I know you wanted to go back the way the sheriff had instructed."

"What can I say? I guess you're just intimidating," he quipped.

He was close to a foot taller than she was. Even if he weren't, she couldn't visualize Clint being intimidated by anyone or anything. That just wasn't in the rancher's nature.

"Yeah, right," she laughed.

She saw a smile curve just the corners of his mouth a moment before she and Clint walked into the diner. "Well, you are," he told her matter-of-factly.

Wynona wasn't sure what came over her.

Maybe it was the triumphant feeling that was all but vibrating through her because they had found Tyler and brought him back to his worried parents. Maybe it was that Clint's smile, unconsciously sexy, had struck a kindred chord deep within her.

Or maybe, just for the moment, she was responding to a man she'd done her very best *not* to respond to from the first moment she had climbed over his fence and walked straight toward him.

Whatever the reason behind her actions, Wynona didn't waste any time analyzing it. She just reacted.

Grabbing hold of the front of Clint's shirt, she stopped him in his tracks and then she turned him toward her.

Before he could ask her what the hell she thought she was doing, she did it.

She kissed him.

Kissed him with all the unbridled emotion that was currently throbbing in her veins.

Had the woman blasted him point-blank with a shotgun, Clint thought that she couldn't have surprised him any more than she did.

Stunned, Clint didn't have time to think about what was going down. Instead, he just reacted the same as she did. Reacted like a suffocating man who had suddenly been connected to a tank of oxygen just mere seconds before he was officially pronounced dead.

Instincts that he had thought had been laid to rest permanently cracked through the invisible walls that he had carefully kept around himself these past seven years and suddenly took over.

He pulled Wynona to him, his arms closing tightly around her as he kissed her back, deepening the unplanned contact.

Without giving it any thought, he lost himself in the heat that had suddenly ignited in his veins, very nearly setting him on fire.

Just as she almost did.

Clint wasn't sure just how long the kiss continued. The only thing he knew was that this woman had managed to awaken things within him that he'd talked himself into believing were dead and that he was better off because they were.

But they weren't dead.

And neither was he.

When Wynona finally drew back—because she was the one who ended the kiss, not him—he found himself staring at her as if he had suddenly been struck mute. Clint struggled to get his bearings.

Struggled to appear unaffected even though he knew in his gut that he wasn't going to fool her. It didn't take a genius to know that she had to have felt him kissing her back.

Attack was always better than retreat. So he did. "What the hell was that?" he asked.

Rather than becoming defensive, he watched, almost in fascination, as a smile blossomed on her lips.

Not one of those self-satisfied or self-congratulating smiles that reeked of smugness, but a smile that radiated happiness. As if she was genuinely happy that he had felt something, the same as she did.

"If you have to ask, Clint," she told him, "then it's been even longer for you than it's been for me."

Clint cleared his throat. He didn't want her thinking that. "No, I just—"

The door to the diner reopened just then and this time it was Miss Joan who was on the top step, one fisted hand at her waist as she looked at them. The fact that she was there herself instead of one of her waitresses was not wasted on them.

"Just how much of a personal invitation do you two need?" Miss Joan asked. "Do I have to get the Murphy brothers to carry you into my establishment?" she asked, referring to the three men who were joint owners of the town's only saloon. "The only way I got them to come here in the first place was to say that this was going to be in your honor. They even donated beer for the occasion," she added.

It was a known fact that Miss Joan and the Murphys had agreed, years ago, that they wouldn't serve meals in their establishment and in return Miss Joan had said that she would not serve spirits in hers. Neither of them had ever violated that agreement.

"They donated beer?" Clint repeated.

He was stalling. Stalling as he desperately

tried to clear his brain so that he could come up with a decent excuse why he couldn't attend this impromptu celebration Miss Joan was throwing.

Right now it felt to him like a fog had descended over his brain, completely blotting out his ability to think.

"That's what it says on the cases they brought with them."

Hazel-green eyes went from Wynona to Clint and then back again.

The knowing look on Miss Joan's face testified that she knew more about what was going on between them than she pretended to. The act was strictly for their benefit, not hers.

"So, are you two coming in or what?" she asked. She didn't bother hiding the impatience in her voice.

Wynona exchanged looks with Clint. Her heart was pounding so hard, she was afraid that Miss Joan would hear it. Most likely, the older woman would be able to see her throat throbbing.

She didn't know why the woman wasn't saying anything about what she had walked in on—Wynona was positive that the woman had seen them kissing—but she was really grateful to Miss Joan for choosing to refrain from making a comment.

Taking a breath, Wynona murmured, "Then I guess we'd better go in. Right, Clint?" It wasn't an order, but a request, asking him to agree with her.

Wynona held the breath she had just taken, hoping that Clint would follow her lead and just go into the diner. If he didn't, she had no doubt that Miss Joan *would* say something, not just to make Clint agree to come into the diner and join the others already there, but also to let him know that she had seen what they had just done. She also had no doubts that Miss Joan would comment on what she had seen.

She really didn't want that out there. At least, not tonight.

"Right," she heard Clint say. And then, as she watched, she saw him follow Miss Joan into the noisy diner.

Only then did Wynona release the breath she was holding.

She hardly felt her feet as she walked in behind Clint.

Chapter Fourteen

Because it looked as if the diner was going to be so crowded, Clint assumed that he could just slip in, and subsequently out again shortly thereafter totally unnoticed.

Instead, the moment he and Wynona walked into the place Miss Joan presided over like a somewhat benevolent empress, they instantly became the center of attention. All the people within the establishment stopped talking, as well as what they were doing, and within seconds a round of applause swept through-out the restaurant until it swelled, becoming a wave that quickly encompassed everyone.

"I guess there's no escaping now, Clint Washburn," Wynona said, smiling up at him.

If it was humanly possible, Clint looked even more uncomfortable now than he had when he first began to cross the threshold.

He probably would have fled, except for the fact that every avenue of escape was blocked by at least two or more human obstacles. There was nowhere to go.

"Relax," Miss Joan whispered, coming up behind him. "There are worse things in life than being regarded as a hero."

Clint didn't want to be "regarded" at all. All he ever wanted to do was to continue going about his life unnoticed.

"How did you know where to find Tyler?" someone called out from within the crowd.

Sensing how very uncomfortable Clint was right now, Wynona answered for him.

"We really didn't know. We just continued searching through the quadrant of the area we were assigned." Seeing that the crowd wanted more, she elaborated. "We thought that Tyler might have looked for shelter in a cave or just about anywhere that would provide him with some kind of protection away from the elements."

She glanced toward the man next to her. "Clint remembered that there were burrows in the area, so we checked them out. And that's where we found Tyler, in the last burrow," she concluded with a smile just as someone pushed a mug of beer into her hands.

"Had to be more to it than that," Garrett Murphy insisted.

"Maybe a little more," Wynona allowed. "But right now I think we're both just too tired to remember the details." Her smile widened. "The point is, Tyler's back with his parents."

"But—" Another Forever resident protested, trying to get more of the story out of one or the other of the heroes.

That was when Miss Joan intervened, moving into the middle of the discussion. She eyed Liam Murphy, another one of the three brothers. "You heard them," the woman said authoritatively, "Wynona said they were tired. Back off, Murphy, or I'll cut you off from your own beer," she warned.

Liam inclined his head. "Yes, ma'am," he said, raising his hands to show that he was surrendering to the inevitable. There was no shame in that. Everyone knew that Miss Joan always won.

Clint appeared rather impressed that despite the legend that existed about her, the thin, at times downright fragile-looking woman could cast such a powerful, almost intimidating shadow.

At this point, Wynona took the opportunity to lean into him.

"You don't have to stay too long," she told Clint, her voice low as she whispered the words into his ear, not wanting to be overheard by anyone else. "You just have to stay long enough to let people thank you."

Clint was intrigued by her reasoning. She made it sound as if it was all him and they both knew that it wasn't.

"You were part of it, too," he told her. "You were *more* than part of it, really. If it weren't for you, I would have turned back," Clint informed her in a quiet voice.

"No, you wouldn't have," she countered knowingly.

He felt Wynona's breath skim along his neck

and cheek as she spoke. Felt a shiver skimming through him in response that he had to consciously tamp down.

This was *not* the time to react to the woman. Actually, there *was* no right time to react to the woman. He'd sworn to himself that he was done with that sort of thing. Allowing himself to react only led to complications he wanted no part of.

"You claiming to know me better than I know myself?" he challenged. The woman hardly knew him at all.

Wynona's mouth curved and he felt her smile curling its way through his insides even as he struggled to try to block it.

"Maybe I do," Wynona answered.

Before he could say anything, Wynona's cousin descended on them, placing a hand on either of their shoulders. Shania's eyes were sparkling as she said, "I knew if anyone could find that boy, you would."

It wasn't clear to Clint if Shania was talking to just her cousin, or if her comment was meant for both of them. Whatever the case, he did what he could to shift the emphasis strictly onto Wynona.

"She insisted on going on even after it grew too dark to be able to see more than a few feet in front of us," he told Shania.

Shania nodded, pride evident in her voice as well as in her smile. "Wynona's always been pushy like that. I'd watch my step if I were you," she added, this time looking directly at him.

Clint frowned. Was she actually making some kind of reference about them actually being a couple? His back went up.

"Why would I have to—"

Clint never got to finish his question, or to voice a denial.

Interrupting him again, Shania laughed as she winked at him. "Just know that forewarned is forearmed," she told him. "I'll leave you two to mingle with your adoring fans." And with that, Wynona's cousin quickly slipped away.

Wynona saw that Clint was frowning again. It struck her almost as odd that he looked rather cute when he did that.

"I don't want to mingle," he protested, although she noticed that he wasn't just walking out of the diner, either.

"I think that's been taken out of your hands," Wynona pointed out. But then she added once again, "Give this just a little longer."

As far as he was concerned, he'd already given this more time than he'd intended. But because he didn't want to cause a scene—

or argue with Miss Joan—he resigned himself to remaining at the celebration "a little longer" as Wynona had suggested.

But *just* a little longer, Clint underscored in his mind.

The crowd gathered around them seemed to have other ideas.

Everyone wanted to buy them a drink, or at least share in the moment with them. Everyone, apparently, appeared to be flying high on a combination of good will and good feelings.

So they stayed longer.

It was only several hours later that Wynona finally offered up an exit excuse that was acceptable to the good citizens of Forever.

"Tomorrow is a school day and I need to get some sleep if I'm going to be of any use to my students," she declared, her words making the rounds in a general fashion. Specifically, Wynona's excuse provided Clint with a reason that allowed him to detach himself from the festivities, as well.

"I'll take you home." The words came out of Clint's mouth before he fully realized just what he was saying or the significance that others might very well wind up attaching to them.

The full import of his words was communicated when Wynona looked at him in surprise.

A beat later the surprised expression melted into a smile as she responded, "That's very nice of you."

He'd gotten caught in a trap inadvertently of his own making, Clint thought as he mumbled, "Yeah, sure." Then, because he couldn't think of anything else to say or any way to get out of this gracefully without looking like a complete idiot, he retorted, "You ready?"

She glanced over to where her cousin was standing. Shania was talking to one of the searchers, a Navajo. Will had come from the reservation when the call had gone out to look for Tyler.

Shania's eyes met hers for a brief moment. They'd always had their own way of communicating and now was no different. Shania nodded at her with a smile, then went back to talking to the native tracker.

"I'm ready," Wynona said, returning her attention back to Clint.

Resigned to playing the Boy Scout, Clint held the door open for her as she walked out of the diner. Wynona smiled at him.

But once they were outside and the door closed behind them, Wynona turned toward the rancher and said, "You don't really have to take me home."

Confusion creased his brow. "But you just said you wanted me to take you home."

"No," Wynona contradicted, "I was just providing you with an excuse to leave the celebration the way you've been *itching* to do since before we ever walked into the diner."

Clint regarded this puzzle of a woman as they went down the steps. Was she saying she didn't want him to take her home? No, that wasn't it. She actually did think she'd provided him with an excuse.

His car was still parked in front of the elementary school where he'd left it when he'd gone to invite her to dinner at the ranch. Taking hold of her elbow, he guided Wynona in that direction now.

"I can make my own excuses," he told her, then added firmly, "I said I was taking you home so I'm taking you home."

Wynona squared her shoulders. "I'm a big girl—" she began.

He thought of the way she'd turned and kissed him just before he'd walked into the diner. A wave of warmth washed over him.

"I'm well aware of that," he assured her.

His voice suddenly sounded silky, almost seductive, Wynona thought. And she could feel him looking at her, his eyes moving over every inch of her very slowly.

It was all she could do not to react.

Forcing herself to focus, Wynona tried again. "What I'm trying to say is that I'm very capable of walking myself home."

He had set ideas when it came to certain things. He was the man and as such, the protector in this scenario. "It's dark." He assumed that was enough to get his point across.

"Very observant," Wynona remarked, the corners of her mouth curving.

He strove for patience. "What I'm saying," he told her, enunciating each word, "is that I'd feel better if I got you home safe."

Her brow furrowed just a little as she looked at him. "Why?"

Clint could feel the last of his patience flying out the window. "Damn it, woman, is everything up for debate with you?"

"I'm just trying to understand you." She wasn't being flippant, just giving an honest answer.

It wasn't an answer that he wanted. She was trying to get close to him and he didn't want that. The very idea scared him.

"Well, don't," he snapped. "Not everything has to be dissected, least of all me."

She looked into his eyes. "What are you afraid of, Clint?"

"That I'll strangle you and they'll convict me," he retorted.

Wynona laughed then. It was a light, silvery sound that undid every single nerve ending in his body, leaving him defenseless.

They were right in front of the school now. He didn't really have any recollection of what came over him. All he knew was that one moment he was walking next to her, the next minute he had her in his arms with his lips pressed against hers.

For the first time in over two hours, he felt like he had come alive again.

Which was all wrong, he silently argued, because he shouldn't be feeling that way.

Shouldn't be doing this.

Shouldn't be *wanting* to do this. But yet, he couldn't stop.

So what he did was try to assure himself that this would never happen again. The only way he felt he could achieve that was to frighten her into keeping her distance. And that would have to involve kissing her so hard, so thoroughly, that the whole experience would wind up leaving an indelible mark on her soul and cause her to run from him. It would be the only way she could save herself.

The only way that *he* could save himself.

The only problem with his plan was that, within moments, he wound up falling into his own trap. Because he wound up kissing Wynona so completely that he was left gasping for air with his head spinning and his heart racing so hard, for a moment he was certain that it was going to burst right through his veins.

Wynona couldn't catch her breath, couldn't get her bearings. Within seconds of his lips covering hers with such feeling, she found that she had lost all orientation. She had no idea where she was.

All she knew was that she didn't want this to stop.

If the world would suddenly come to an end right at this very moment, this was exactly the way she would have wanted to die because this was truly the most wonderful thing she had *ever* experienced.

There was no improving on perfection.

When Clint finally drew back, looking, she thought, as overwhelmed and disoriented as she felt, neither one of them could speak.

And then, as the silence stretched out, underscored by the pounding of her heart echoing in her ears, Wynona heard herself saying breathlessly, "I don't live very far from here." She had to concentrate on breathing. "Would you like to come over?"

Was she asking what he thought she was asking—or was he just hoping that she was?

No, damn it, Clint silently argued, he didn't

want this to happen, didn't want to sink into that quicksand again, feeling as if he had lost his very soul. His life was simple now. It was straightforward. He knew exactly what to expect from each day. No surprises. Feelings only complicated that.

And yet you're feeling really alive for the first time in years, a small voice in his head whispered.

His mouth felt almost dry as he finally answered her question. "I shouldn't."

Wynona shook her head. "That's not what I asked," she told him quietly. Her eyes on his as she repeated her question. "Do you *want* to come over?"

All he had to do was say no then turn on his heel and walk away—after he brought her home. That was what he'd said he was going to do and he wasn't, as she had pointed out with great emphasis, a man who didn't honor his word.

But once he brought Wynona up to her door, he knew that he would go inside if she invited him. If she *asked* him to, he thought.

If.

The single word vibrated in his mind, almost mocking him.

"It's not that difficult a question," Wynona told him, her voice soft, almost seductive, as she waited for him to say something. "*Do* you want to?" she asked Clint for a third time.

It felt as if time had suddenly stood still.

He tried; he really tried to say the word. Tried to say no to her and with that at least temporarily put an end to his anguish.

After all, turning her down was the honorable thing to do. The *right* thing to do.

But as Clint looked down into her upturned face, Wynona's brilliant blue eyes all but mesmerizing him, he heard himself say the word that would, in all likelihood, wind up sealing his doom.

He said the word so quietly it was almost too quiet to be heard.

But she heard it anyway.

"Yes."

Chapter Fifteen

He really didn't remember the short drive to Wynona's house.

It felt like one moment he was opening the passenger door for her, waiting until she had seated herself and buckled up, the next moment he was pulling up his vehicle, bringing it to a stop before the modest house where she and her cousin currently lived. Everything in between had been just a big blur.

Clint made his way around the rear of his

truck on legs that felt as if they were on loan from someone else. Coming to her side of the truck he put his hand on the passenger door handle.

Independent to a fault, Wynona had always felt that she was perfectly capable of getting out of the truck by herself. She nearly started to tell him as much.

But she sensed that all these steps were somehow important to Clint so she restrained her natural inclination to just climb out un-aided and waited for him to open the door.

When he did, she was careful to take the hand he offered her before she stepped out. Her heart was beating wildly. Her eyes never left his face.

"We're here," he told her in a voice she couldn't quite fathom.

"We are," she agreed as if to rubber-stamp

his words. She turned from him and unlocked her front door.

The sound of the lock clicking open seemed somehow magnified in the stillness.

She pushed the door open, then walked into the small, welcoming house.

Clint wasn't following her.

He wasn't debating the wisdom of coming into her house; he already knew that came under the heading of a foolish move even though he knew he was going to make it. What Clint was doing was attempting to reconcile himself with the consequences that he was certain were waiting for him once what he was about to do came to its logical conclusion.

Crossing the threshold, Wynona quickly moved about the living room, turning on lights, trying to make the house seem less intimate.

Once the room was sufficiently illuminated, she turned around to see if Clint had come in yet.

He hadn't.

Facing him, Wynona said nothing. She just stood there and waited in silence.

"It's warmer once you come in and close the door," she coaxed.

"Yeah," he agreed belatedly. Then taking in one more long breath, he walked into the house and closed the door behind him with his back.

Okay, Wynona thought. *Part one is over.* "Can I get you something to drink?" she asked.

For a second, Clint's mind went completely blank. Regaining the use of his tongue, he heard himself asking, "What do you have?"

Wynona moved toward the refrigerator. "Well, let's see." Opening the door she began to move things around to see what was available inside. "Looks like we have orange juice, beer, red wine and soda," she enumerated. "I can put up a pot of coffee if you like," she offered, straightening up and turning to look in his direction. "What's your pleasure?"

Only then did she realize that Clint had crossed the room over to her. He was now all but toe to toe with her, looking down into her face.

"You." The response was automatic without any deliberation or thought from him.

Trying to remember to breathe, Wynona released the refrigerator door, pushing it shut.

"Then I guess you're in luck," she answered. "I just happen to have some of that on hand."

Before she could berate herself for giving voice to a totally mindless answer, Clint had caught her up in his arms and brought his mouth down on hers.

The heat, the combustion between them, was instant, firing her up and setting Wynona off like a flare shooting up into the darkened night sky.

She kissed him back as hard, and with as much feeling, as he had kissed her. This part of her life had been untapped for a very long time but there was no working her way up to passion. It was right there, waiting to be set off. One spark and it was engulfing her.

Desire took over.

Wynona couldn't just focus on any one area or on any one thing. Every part of her was responding. Every part of her was vibrating with excitement.

His lips roamed all over her face, her neck, branding every inch of skin as he came in contact with it.

Moving lower.

And just when she thought that there was no

turning back, no stopping this runaway train that was barreling down the track, going full steam ahead, Clint pulled back, stunning her.

Wynona pressed her lips together to suppress the moan, the protest that had risen to her lips. Regaining her breath was a challenge as confusion ran rampant through her brain.

He couldn't be stopping now—could he?

"What's wrong?" she asked Clint, doing what she could to steady her breathing so that she wouldn't sound as if she was gasping for air.

"Your cousin," he responded, the two words just hanging in the air between them.

It was enough.

She understood.

It stunned her that he was that aware, that thoughtful of her at a time that was so fraught with emotion. In essence, he was thinking of the effect this would have on her reputation.

He was putting it—and thus her—ahead of his own needs.

"She won't be home for a few hours," Wynona assured him, praying that the momentary pause in the midst of all this wouldn't cause him to change his mind and make him go home.

Clint leaned in and kissed her again, but not with as much frenzied passion as he'd exhibited just a moment ago. She felt a sinking sensation in the pit of her stomach.

Had he had a change of heart? Was he leaving after all?

If he had an ounce of sense in his head, Clint would leave rather than allow this hollow longing within him to drive him this way.

But there *wasn't* enough sense and there was far too much hollow longing driving him onward—no, *begging* him to go onward.

"Where's your bedroom?" he asked Wynona in a raspy voice.

He wasn't leaving!

She almost cheered out loud as she took hold of his hand. Turning around, she led the way from the kitchen toward the two rooms that were beyond it.

Hers was the one on the right side.

The moment they were inside the room, closing the door on the rest of the world, Clint pulled her back into his arms again.

Kissed her again as if his very life depended on the action.

Clint had her up against the wall, kissing her with every shred of passion that had been totally unleashed within him.

She could feel his heart racing as his chest pressed up against hers.

This time there would be no turning back, no hesitation. She could *feel* it.

Her head was swimming as the depth of his kisses grew, engulfing her. Stealing away the very air out of her lungs.

She didn't care.

All she cared about was that Clint was here, with her. He was making everything within her sizzle with the force of a hundred suns.

Wynona struggled to make this taciturn man feel every single thing that she was feeling. She *needed* to make him feel what she was feeling.

Someone had ripped this man's heart out without a second thought, paralyzing all of his emotions. She was determined to bring him back among the living. And just as determined not to make him regret the fact that he could feel again.

Their lips sealed together, they tumbled onto her bed, caught up in absorbing every sensation, every nuance, that was being stirred and brought back to life.

She felt his hands on her body, caressing her, possessing her and pulling aside the cloth barriers that were in his way.

She felt her clothes being removed from her body, being cast aside. As warm breath covered her body, it instantly prompted her to follow suit, undressing Clint with movements that were more jagged than fluid.

Even so, she still managed to do the job.

And then they were both nude.

Their bodies tangling together as if there was no question that this was what had been intended all along since the very beginning of time.

The voice of reason that Clint had cultivated over the years until it was almost all he was aware of had begun to fade from the first moment their lips had met. The voice was almost totally submerged now, melted in the bubbling waters of desire.

In a last-ditch attempt, he tried to summon it, to resurrect it. But it was completely out of reach, almost totally gone.

He didn't want to stop, didn't want to think. He just wanted this all-encompassing, addictive feeling shooting through his body to be allowed free rein until that was all there was within him.

The sensation was too overwhelming for him to release from his grip. It had been far too long since he had felt like an actual human being instead of just an empty shell.

Wynona twisted and turned beneath him, surrendering to Clint even as she held him captive. She moaned as his hot mouth skimmed along the length of her, leaving her almost completely mindless, a throbbing mass of hungry desire.

With her last shred of strength, she struggled to do the same to him. To make him *feel* the way she did.

Her pulse racing, she felt that she had succeeded, at least in part.

For a man who had withdrawn from the land of the living for so many years, he was unbelievably incredible, Wynona thought, making every single inch of her sing even as she longed for the final fulfilling moment, for the explosion that promised to rock her entire world.

Instinctively, she knew that it wasn't an empty promise. The only reason a part of her was still striving to hang back was because she wanted this feeling to go on for as long as possible.

But her self-control was splintering. Within

moments she no longer had the strength to hold him—and herself—at bay.

She *needed* to feel that enormous final rush seizing her in its powerful grip.

Wynona arched her back, her body moving temptingly beneath his. With her eyes silently on his expression, she parted her legs, her invitation clear.

Clint's heart was pounding so hard, he could barely see straight.

Gathering her into his arms as she lay beneath him, his eyes never left her. Everything stood still as he entered her.

The instant he did, she began to move, her body urging him on to that one final place where they could complete each other.

With each passing moment, her tempo increased. Clint moved faster.

She upped the pace and he was right there,

keeping up with her and then increasing the tempo until they were both so swept up in it, nothing else mattered.

This went on until they were both moving so fast, it was difficult to know who was outdistancing whom. Or if it even mattered.

The final gratifying explosion seized them simultaneously, enveloping them in a euphoria that defied description.

Clint realized that he was holding on to her tightly, not wanting this to end. Knowing that the moment he stopped holding her so close to him, it would.

The wild pounding of his heart lessened by increments until it was almost back to normal.

Normal was no longer a good thing, he thought. Normal was barren. Lonely. And he had no desire to move back into that stark prison.

Not yet.

He felt Wynona move against him, her torso radiating warmth as she shifted. In the next instant her body was partially over his.

And then she raised her head, the smile on her lips somehow leeching into his very consciousness. That he was aware of it surprised him. That he liked it surprised him even more.

"Bet when you came to school to invite me to the ranch for dinner you never thought we'd wind up like this at the end of the day," she said.

He had no idea why that struck him so funny, but it did and he laughed. At first, a little and then whole-heartedly.

The laughter in his chest transferred itself to her, turning into something they felt jointly.

"No," he agreed, stroking her hair as he finally caught his breath, "I can't say that I did."

Wynona shifted again. He felt her breasts moving against his chest. Felt himself get-

ting aroused all over again. Despite the vig-
orous, all but draining, lovemaking they had
just experienced, somehow he found himself
wanting her all over again.

He had to be losing his mind. But it wasn't
his mind that was causing his body to respond
this way.

He could feel her smile on his skin as it
spread along her lips. The next second she
was raising her head again.

"Again?" she asked.

Considering their state of undress, there was
no hiding his reaction to her. But he didn't
want her thinking that he was some insatia-
ble creature who would demand satisfaction
from her whether she was up to it or not.

"No, I—"

He didn't get a chance to finish. Wynona
wiggled her body even closer to his, her eyes
sparkling with humor and laughter.

"Again," she repeated.

This time he didn't hear it as a question. This time, he realized, she was telling him what *she* wanted.

But was she just saying that to go along with what she could tell he wanted? He shifted farther in order to be able to squarely face her.

"You sure?"

As she leaned in to kiss him, Clint could feel the laughter on her lips. When she moved her head back, creating a small space, her smile had widened, spreading from ear to ear.

"What do you think?"

"I think the best is yet to come," he answered, the words all but vibrating within him as they emerged on his lips.

"My thoughts exactly." Her eyes were bright with laughter as she raised her lips to his.

Chapter Sixteen

Had she made a mistake?

Had leaving the celebration at Miss Joan's diner and bringing Clint home with her been ultimately a mistake on her part?

Wynona didn't want to believe that, but as each day passed, fading into the next, she began to grow more and more certain that, no matter what was in her heart, she had made a mistake.

Making love with Clint had felt so right

when it was happening. She had been sure that deep down inside him, he was feeling the exact same thing that she was. Moreover, that Clint had feelings for her just the way she had for him.

But after they'd made love—*twice*—he had quickly gotten dressed and left, making a point of leaving before Shania came home.

At the time she had thought that Clint was just being protective of her. That he didn't want her cousin to know that they had slept together until and unless she was the one who wanted to tell Shania about them.

But she was beginning to think that maybe he hadn't wanted Shania to know—hadn't wanted *anyone* to know—not because he was protecting her but because making love with her hadn't really meant anything to him. That what had happened was all just part of an age-old cliché.

Now that Clint had gotten what he'd wanted from her, she no longer mattered to him.

With all her heart, Wynona didn't want to believe that, but what other explanation was there for his disappearing act?

Two weeks had gone by and she hadn't heard a word from Clint. He had made no attempt to get in contact with her in order to finalize any plans regarding having dinner at the ranch. He hadn't called, hadn't even sent a message to her via his son.

Nothing.

It was as if now that he'd slept with her, he no longer wanted any part of her.

Had she just imagined the whole thing? Imagined that he cared?

Wynona had no idea what to think. All she knew was that her heart ached and it was all because of Clint.

She was able to keep up a brave face in

class, but it was getting a little more difficult with each day that passed.

"When is Miss Chee going to come over for dinner?" Ryan asked his father.

The boy had waylaid him by the corral to ask the question.

This time.

The boy had asked him the same question every day for over two weeks ever since the afternoon that he had gone into town to extend the invitation to Wynona and gotten caught up in the search for Tyler.

Gotten caught up in Wynona, Clint thought almost unwillingly.

Making love with the woman had been nothing short of exquisite. It also showed him how very susceptible he was to her. Showed him in no uncertain terms how extremely *vul-*

nerable he was when it came to anything that had to do with Wynona.

And that scared him.

Scared him because since he felt the way he did about her, it gave the woman power over him. The kind of power that could, so very easily, completely undo him.

Completely destroy him.

The last time that had happened, he had managed, through sheer grit, to pull himself together. To resurrect himself out of the ashes that Susan had reduced his soul to when she had coldly walked out on him and their son without so much as a word. Without any kind of warning.

But he instinctively knew that if that happened to him again, there wouldn't be anything left of him to rise up again.

His gut told him that he wouldn't be able to survive a death blow like that.

So for his son's sake, as well as his own, Clint decided that he needed to cut off all ties with Wynona *now* before his inner constitution dissolved to the point that he didn't have the strength to walk away. Because if he didn't cut off all ties, if he wound up convincing himself that he could maintain at least minimal contact with her and still be able to keep his distance emotionally, then he was utterly doomed.

No, cutting off all connection with the woman was the only way that he had even a prayer of remaining whole and sane.

Knowing that didn't make its execution easy. If anything, the complete opposite was true.

And having Ryan constantly asking him about the invitation, about when Wynona was coming over to the house, really didn't help.

"I don't know," Clint finally said when he felt his son's eyes all but boring into him.

"But you said you were gonna ask her," Ryan reminded him innocently. "That was two weeks ago," the boy pointed out, then paused as he thought about it. "More," he corrected. He looked at his father hopefully, obviously trying to push him along without coming right out saying as much. "Miss Chee said yesterday that it's never polite to keep anyone waiting."

Clint's eyes narrowed as he looked up from the repair work he was doing.

"Oh she did, did she?" He could feel his walls going up, bent on securing his heart in place so that it would be safe from the painful consequences of any verbal assault.

Had he been right in his estimation of the woman? Was she fighting dirty by using his own son against him? "Did she say that to you specifically?"

Ryan looked at him in confusion. "No, she said that to the class, but—"

"So she was just talking in general," Clint retorted curtly, terminating the conversation. His cold, stern tone warned his son not to say anything further on the subject.

The message was not received. Except for the bottom line, which told Ryan that the invitation hadn't been delivered.

"But, Dad, why can't she come to our house?" Ryan asked plaintively.

This new stubborn streak Ryan was displaying was a revelation to him. Where was this coming from? Clint wondered, irritated.

Exasperated and at a loss how to answer Ryan, Clint fell back on an old stand-by.

"Don't you have some homework to do?" he asked.

Ryan's face fell. "Yes, but—"

"Then go do it," Clint snapped at his son, turning back to his work.

Ryan made one more attempt to get his father to see things his way. "But, Dad—"

He got no further.

Clint's eyes darkened as he looked sternly at his son. "Now," he ordered.

Ryan dropped his head and walked slowly back to the house, taking baby steps as if he were part of a funeral procession.

Only once the boy was out of earshot did Roy step out of the stable and cross over to where his brother was standing.

"A little hard on the boy, weren't you, Clint?" he asked.

Clint was in no mood to be on the receiving end of a lecture, especially not from his brother. Roy had never been in any kind of a serious relationship and had no idea what he was going through.

With a careless shrug, Clint looked back at his work. "He's got to learn."

Roy moved around until he was right in front of his brother. "Learn what?" he asked. "That his father, the hero, is as unapproachable as ever?"

Clint glared at his brother. "I'm not a hero," he snapped.

"Keep shutting Ryan out like that and you damn well won't be," Roy agreed. Clint made no attempt to explain his actions, leaving Roy no choice but to demand, "What the hell's come over you?"

"Nothing," Clint retorted. He just wanted everyone to leave him alone. But apparently, Roy wasn't taking the hint. Glaring at his younger brother, Clint told him, "Look, if you don't have anything to do, I can find work for you."

Roy ignored the offer, seeing it as nothing but an attempt to divert him from what was really wrong with his brother. "You've been behaving like a wounded bear ever since the night you and Wynona found that boy and brought him back." Roy's eyes widened as a thought suddenly occurred to him. "Something happened between you and that teacher, didn't it?"

"No!" Clint shouted.

The sound of his voice registered and Clint abruptly closed his mouth, moving over to another section of the corral.

Roy refused to let him walk away. "Yes, it did," he insisted, the pieces finally all coming together for him. "Hot damn, you came back to the world of the living and made love with Wynona, didn't you?"

His hand tightening on his hammer, Clint shot his brother a dirty look as he drove the nail into the post with far more vigor than was required. All the while he kept his mouth shut.

But Roy wouldn't give up or be put off. Grinning, he clamped his hand on his older brother's shoulder, taking Clint's silence as affirmation. "Wow, that's wonderful, Clint."

Clint's look grew even darker. "What's so wonderful about it?" he demanded angrily.

"It means you can feel," Roy emphasized, still rejoicing in what he took to be his brother's reawakening.

Clint was quick to set him straight. "Well, I don't want to feel," he ground out between clenched teeth.

Momentarily taken aback, Roy could only look at his older brother in confusion. And then his confusion slowly receded as he smiled again. "I think it's too late, Clint. You already do."

Clint had had just about enough of his brother's babbling. "You have no idea what you're talking about. And no, I don't." He paused for a second, then told his brother with even more feeling, "I *won't*."

"Why?" Roy asked.

"Because I am not going to go through that again," Clint insisted even more angrily, walking away from his brother again.

"Go through what again?" Roy asked, following him. He refused to just give up and walk away from Clint. This was far too important; Clint had to realize that, he thought. "Being in love?"

Clint whirled around. "No! Being ripped to shreds," he snapped.

"Who's ripping you to shreds?" Roy asked in all innocence. "Wynona?" he guessed, then asked in disbelief, "Has she done something to you?"

Another man would have said yes and been done with it. But he had to be honest even though he just wanted Roy to go away and leave him alone. "Not yet."

"Oh. Then all this—" he circled his hand around in front of Clint "—this building up of walls around yourself again, that's just you taking preventative measures, is that it?"

The last shred of his temper went up in smoke. "Back off! It's none of your damn business," Clint shouted.

But Roy wasn't about to back off, not this time. Clint was hurting and it was time to put a stop to it.

"You're my brother. It damn well *is* my business. And this my-heart's-made-of-stone act of yours is hurting your son, so that would make it my business even if I *wasn't* your brother, understand?" Roy demanded. He was close to losing his own temper because he couldn't seem to knock any sense into his brother's thick head.

"How?" Clint demanded. "How is this hurting my son? This is between Wynona and me."

Roy laughed drily as he shook his head. "You keep telling yourself that."

"Why?" Clint repeated. He didn't see how this could have any repercussions on his son, unless Roy meant Wynona would retaliate as Ryan's teacher. "She wouldn't take this out on him," he protested. Wynona wasn't like that, Clint thought.

"No, she wouldn't and she isn't," Roy agreed. "But you are."

Roy had lost him again. Clint had no idea what his brother was talking about. "No, I'm not."

"Oh no?" Roy questioned, then proceeded to give Clint examples. "You're pushing him away, snarling at him like a wounded bear. No wonder Ryan thinks he's done something wrong."

Clint was stunned. How could Roy say that? "I never said that to him," Clint insisted.

"Maybe not in so many words," Roy allowed, "but Ryan's filling in the blanks. Kids always think they've done something wrong when their parent snaps at them."

Roy stood studying his brother, waiting to see if he'd gotten through the thick shields that Clint had constructed around himself.

When Clint continued to remain silent, saying nothing in response, Roy tried again. This time, in a quiet voice, he said, "She's not going to do it, you know."

Clint's head snapped up. He didn't have to

ask who the "she" was that Roy was referring to. He knew. "Do what?"

"If you're waiting for Wynona to walk out on you because she's looking for something more fulfilling in her life, she's not going to do it," Roy told him.

Clint scowled. "You don't know what you're talking about."

Roy continued looking at him. "Did you even take any time to find things out about this woman?" he asked. Not waiting for an answer, he continued, telling his brother what *he* had found out about Wynona. "She grew up on the reservation right outside Forever. While she was in a strong community, life was hard. She never knew her father and lost her mother young. Her uncle and aunt took her in. Things were good for a year and then she lost them, too. The uncle in a car accident and the aunt to pneumonia.

"She and her cousin were minutes away from being swallowed up into the foster care system when her great-aunt suddenly came on the scene and took them both with her to Houston where she lived. She paid for both their college educations. Wynona could have done anything she wanted once she got her teaching degree and all she wanted to do was come back here to show kids that it was possible to become something if they worked hard at it."

Clint said nothing. Frustrated, Roy shouted at his brother. "Don't you get it? Wynona isn't anything like Susan. Susan was the center of her own universe. Wynona is a selfless woman who only wants to help people. She's a rare human being," Roy said with feeling. "So if you don't come to your senses and start acting more like the grown-up you were when you were eighteen instead of the cowering, scared kid that Susan turned you into, then you are *not* the brother I know and I'm ashamed of you."

Clint frowned, although the anger had been all but totally leeched out of him.

"You think you have all the answers, don't you?" he asked.

"No, you do," Roy told him.

This time Clint could only wave a hand dismissively. "Yeah, right."

But Roy wasn't about to be put off. "You do. You just have to look a little harder into yourself. And remember, Wynona isn't Susan. Susan wasn't good enough to even clean Wynona's shoes," he insisted. "Now, I can't tell you what to do—"

"Doesn't seem to be stopping you," Clint commented, the fire having entirely left his voice.

"But if I were you," Roy continued as if he

hadn't been interrupted, "I'd run, not walk, to that teacher's house, fall on my knees in front of her and *beg* her to forgive me."

"I can't do that." He'd done too much damage by staying away. It was already too late for any apologies.

"Yeah, you can," Roy insisted. "You can tell her you'd taken temporary leave of your senses, but you're all better now and you will do *anything* to make it up to her if she would just give you another chance."

Clint laughed drily. "You have this whole thing worked out, don't you?"

Roy became serious as he answered, "All except the part where I get you to listen to reason and try to win her back."

"It's too late for that," Clint repeated. "The damage is done."

"You don't know that," Roy insisted.

"Yeah, I do," Clint answered flatly.

"No, you don't," Roy countered. He could guess what his brother was thinking. "You're afraid she'll turn you down but you don't know for sure. And my money is on Wynona. The woman has a great capacity to overlook people's flaws."

"How do you know that?"

"She was willing to go out with you, wasn't she?" Roy pointed out.

He hadn't told Roy that he'd told Wynona on the night of the search that he had initially sought her out at the school to ask her to come to dinner. "How would you know that?"

"Simple. You don't share anything with me so I make it my job to find things out," Roy explained, adding, "I was never the kind of guy who was content staying in the dark. Now, for the love of Pete, stop stalling! Get into your truck and drive over to her place before someone else in town realizes what a catch that woman is and aces you out of what could have been the best thing that ever happened to you—outside of me and the kid."

The last words were addressed to Clint's back as his brother turned on his heel and began to run toward his truck.

Roy smiled. *Finally!*

There was hope for his brother after all.

Chapter Seventeen

Clint kept going over what he wanted to say to Wynona the entire trip from his ranch to her doorstep. Rehearsing, he used different words each time, predominantly because he couldn't remember the words he'd used only minutes before.

Nothing he said sounded right.

Clint swore under his breath. He'd blown it; he was certain of it. Wynona was never going to give him a second chance, he thought.

And why should she? If he'd been in her place, he certainly wouldn't give him a second chance.

"If you had half a brain in your head, Washburn, you'd just turn around and go home," he told himself in hopeless disgust.

Clint's frown deepened. If he did just turn around and go home, he knew that Roy would give him hell. But that didn't matter to him. Maybe he even deserved it, he thought. But what *had* gotten to him, what kept him driving to town rather than just giving up, turning around and heading back home, was the look he had seen on Ryan's face earlier.

The look he would see again if he returned without having even *tried* to get Wynona to understand why he had done what he'd done.

The look of complete, total disappointment.

Clint sighed. He had finally seen his son coming around, finally becoming lively and animated. He didn't want to be the one responsible for making Ryan revert back to the withdrawn shell of a boy he had been before Wynona had come into their lives.

So he kept driving, ready to take his medicine and whatever else he had to do in order to, as Roy had pointed out, rejoin the forces of the living.

He still didn't know what to say or how to begin.

All the words he had rehearsed on the drive here completely deserted him as he brought his truck to a halt in front of Wynona's house. Deserted him and scurried away like rats fleeing a sinking ship.

He could far more easily face down a wild, bucking mustang than do what he was about to do.

He *knew* what to do when it came to taming

a wild horse. He was good at it. But as far as baring his soul to a woman he knew he was guilty of treating badly—a woman who deserved so much better than him—he had no idea what to say or what to do.

Completely clueless, he had no idea how to make her forgive him. All he knew was that he *wanted* her to forgive him.

Steeling himself off, he finally raised his hand and knocked on the door.

There was no answer at first and he knocked again. Was Wynona still at the school?

Or had she gone out? Maybe she was at Miss Joan's, or—

A number of places crossed his mind and he thought about looking for her, then decided that eventually, the woman who had taught him that he still had a heart had to come home.

Right?

He finally decided he was going to wait for her in his truck no matter how long it took.

Reluctantly turning away from the front of the house, he had just begun to walk to his truck when he heard the door behind him opening.

Clint whirled around immediately, prepared to launch into a disjointed, jumbled apology in order to break down any walls that Wynona might have constructed around herself.

But the words he began to say froze on his lips. He wasn't looking at Wynona. He was looking into the disapproving face of her cousin, Shania.

"Are you lost?" Shania asked him coldly. "The feed store is on the next street," she told him, pointing in the store's general direction.

He wasn't in the habit of making anyone privy to his business, but he knew that wasn't going to cut it right now. Forcing himself to put his personal feelings aside, he told the young woman in the doorway, "I want to talk to Wynona."

Shania remained planted right where she was, blocking any access into the house. She even put her hands on opposite sides of the doorsill to form even more of a barrier.

"Well, she doesn't want to talk to you so why don't you just go back where you came from?" Shania suggested with a smile that was cold enough to freeze a medium-size lake.

He'd come this far; Clint decided to push a little further. "I want to hear Wynona tell me to go."

Shania's face darkened. "You are not in any position to make any demands, Washburn."

"But—" Clint protested.

Shania wasn't about to hear him out. "You lost that right," Shania informed him angrily, "when you treated my cousin as if she didn't matter."

"I need to talk to her, to explain," Clint insisted, refusing to be put off. "Wynona needs to understand that I didn't mean to hurt her."

Shania wasn't budging. "Talk is cheap, Washburn," she retorted.

"Please," Clint said. His eyes said things to Wynona's cousin that he couldn't.

"It's all right, Shania," Wynona said quietly, coming up behind her cousin. She placed a hand on Shania's shoulder. "Let him come in."

Shania frowned. If it was up to her, she'd toss Washburn out on his ear, but ultimately this was Wynona's call.

"Fine," she relented, stepping aside. "I'll go get a broom and a dustpan so I can sweep up the pieces that'll be left behind once he's had his say."

Clint walked in as Shania left the room. The

latter paused to shoot a warning look at him over her shoulder before leaving the area.

"She hates me, doesn't she?" Clint said to Wynona as he closed the door.

Rather than agree with or deny the assessment, Wynona merely said, "She's being protective of me." Hoping she wasn't going to regret this, Wynona led the way into the living room. "Would you like some coffee?" she asked him, turning around.

He had no desire to drink coffee or anything else, but it was a way of stalling for a few minutes, so he said, "Sure, why not?"

"I'll be right back," Wynona replied, then walked into the kitchen.

Shania had put up a pot of fresh coffee when she'd come home earlier and there was still about half a pot left. Wynona poured a cup and returned with it to the living room.

He saw the single cup. "You're not having any?" he questioned.

She shook her head. "If I have coffee past a certain hour, it keeps me up at night."

"Oh." Clint put the cup she had brought him down on the small coffee table, untouched.

"Not to your liking?" she questioned.

The smile on his lips was forced. "I'm sure it's fine."

This whole situation was so awkward, it was downright painful, Wynona thought. It was time to put both of them out of their misery.

"Why are you here, Clint?" she asked him.

Picking up on her tone, he read into it. "Do you want me to leave?"

Wynona didn't say yes or no. Instead, frustrated, she said, "What I want is for you to tell me why you left your ranch, drove all the way here and asked me for a cup of coffee you had no intention of drinking."

"Well, technically," he told her, "I didn't ask for the coffee. You offered it."

Wynona's eyes widened. He was going to lecture her about *technicalities*? Wynona felt her temper spiking. "And 'technically,'" she retorted, "no court in the world would convict me if I threw the cup of coffee straight at your head."

Clint took a breath. "I'm sorry."

"Not as sorry as you're going to be once that cup grazes your skull," she informed him angrily.

She had kept her temper under wraps for the past two and a half weeks, struggling not to allow anyone to glimpse the pain she was going through. Now that she had allowed her temper to finally erupt, she was having trouble getting it back under control.

But Clint didn't let himself get distracted, didn't extrapolate on any sidebars that had come up. Now that he had finally said the words to her, all he could do was repeat them until their meaning sank in with her.

"I'm sorry," he said to Wynona again.

"Well, you just—"

About to make another comment, this one about the way his vanishing act had affected her, Wynona stopped midword and stared at him, her eyes wide. She was reading into this; she just knew it.

But even so, Wynona heard herself asking, "You're what?"

"I'm sorry," Clint repeated a third time with sincerity. "Very, very sorry."

Afraid that she was interpreting his words in her own way, Wynona wanted this apology spelled out.

"For?" she asked him, waiting.

He took in a deep breath as if to fortify himself. And then he said, "For not getting back to you. For acting like a coward. For allowing a ghost from the past to do a number on me and scare me off." Revved up, his words took on strength as he continued. "For very possibly losing the best thing that's happened to me. I've lost sight of the last time I felt so happy. I'm sorry for—"

Wynona put her index finger against his lips, stilling them. Despite everything, she could feel her mouth curving.

"You can stop now. You've answered my question," she told him.

But he had only gotten started. "I know this isn't something a man's supposed to admit," he told Wynona, his voice softening, "but making love with you woke up so many things inside me, things I wanted to feel, I was afraid that you'd use that against me somehow."

She looked at him, feeling both hurt and mystified at his reasoning. "I think that maybe we need to go back to the beginning so that you can get to know me, get to know the kind of person I am."

"I already know you," Clint told her.

But Wynona shook her head. "No, you don't. If you did, you wouldn't have harbored those kinds of thoughts about me. You would have known better."

"That didn't have anything to do with you," he told her with feeling. "All those thoughts had to do with Ryan's mother. When we started out, I had those kinds of feeling about her. She used them to twist my heart right out of my chest like it was some kind of a living corkscrew."

Reliving these memories was incredibly painful, but if he had a prayer of making Wynona stay, he had to share them with her so she could understand what had driven him to do what he'd done.

"When I found that Susan had just up and left me without warning, I thought I'd never recover. Eventually, I learned to live with the pain and I made my peace with that, but I wanted to make sure that it never was going to happen to me again."

She saw it differently. "You were a man with no heart, no feelings, who couldn't even relate to his own son. That's not making your peace with anything, Clint." Couldn't he see that? "That's resigning from life altogether."

He looked at Wynona, looked into her eyes as she spoke. He felt her passion. Moreover, he knew she didn't just have a point; she was completely right.

So he told her as much.

"You're right," Clint said out loud.

Wynona had revved herself up to deliver a full-fledged lecture to him. To have Clint immediately agree took away some of her thunder, leaving her with nothing to add.

She blinked. "I am?"

"Yes," Clint answered. "You are."

"Well, I guess I can't argue with that," Wynona murmured.

A hint of a smile slipped over his lips. Why had he run from this? What kind of an idiot did that make him? "You can if you want to," he told her.

"What I want," she told him, "is to just forget the past two and a half weeks ever happened."

"But not the lovemaking," Clint quickly interjected, looking at her hopefully.

"No," Wynona agreed, smiling at him, "not the lovemaking. Not if it's the part that you *want* to remember." She held her breath, waiting to see what he would say to that.

Her stipulation puzzled him. "Why wouldn't

I want to remember coming to life for the first time in over seven years?" he asked her.

She just wanted to be sure that it was as important to him as it was to her. "I have no idea," she told him honestly. "I never claimed to be able to understand the male mind."

Relieved beyond words that it looked as if it was going to work out after all, Clint put his arms around her. "I could give you a quick course. If you're interested, that is."

"I guess I have to be. That is, if I'm going to survive this relationship." And then, just to make sure she hadn't jumped to conclusions, she asked, "This *is* a relationship, right?"

Clint nodded. "That's one way to describe it," he answered.

She wasn't sure what to make of his response. "What's another way?" she asked, looking at him uncertainly, bracing herself for anything.

He took a breath to fortify himself. "How about 'an engagement?'"

Had she had any of the coffee she had offered him, she would have undoubtedly been choking on it at this point.

As it was, she found herself coughing as she tried to catch her breath. "What did you just say?"

"An engagement," he repeated, then quickly backtracked, afraid he'd taken too much for granted. "No, I'm sorry, that was too soon. I shouldn't have just thrown you into the deep end of the pool like that. I didn't mean to—"

Wynona put her hands on either side of his face, symbolically capturing his words so that he could catch his breath.

"I think you missed a few steps, Clint. Do you want to start from the beginning?" she asked.

"The beginning?" he asked. Then, as she

nodded her head, he said, "Right, the beginning. Do you think that maybe you might, maybe someday, be willing to maybe think about, um, well, marrying me?"

Not exactly the eloquent proposal she was hoping for, Wynona thought. But it would do.

"Someday?" she questioned.

He took that to mean that she thought it was the right word to use in this case.

"Yes, like maybe a long time from now," he added quickly.

"Why?" she asked. She needed to hear reasons, *his* reasons, before she answered the all-important question that was making her heart flutter.

"Why?" he repeated, not sure what she wanted to hear him say.

So she explained it to him. "*Why* are you asking me to marry you?"

"Because I love you," he said, blurting out the answer before he had time to stop himself.

Wynona smiled. Finally. "That's all I wanted to hear," she informed him.

"So does that mean you'll think about it?" he asked hopefully.

Her eyes were dancing as she answered, "Think about it?"

She managed to suppress the laugh that rose up in her throat. The man was going to really have to work on his confidence, she thought. Couldn't he see that she loved him?

"No, I'm not going to think about it. I'm going to say yes, you big, thick-headed cowboy. Because I love you," she told him before he could ask.

Relieved beyond words, Clint pulled her into his arms. Lord, but she felt good, he couldn't help thinking. A part of him had been convinced that he'd lost her. He had never been so happy to be wrong.

"I love you, too," he said, lowering his mouth to hers.

The rest of what happened after that was a blur, but that was all right with them. After all, they had the rest of their lives to sort it all out.

Epilogue

Clint was standing in one of the two tiny rooms located at the rear of the church. The rooms were reserved for brides and bridegrooms spending their final moments as single people just before they exchanged the vows that would bind them to each other.

At the moment, he was looking into the full-length mirror and doing his best to get his tie straight. In his opinion, the gunmetal-gray suit he was wearing made him look as if he had just fallen off the top of a wedding cake, but he wasn't doing this for himself. He was doing this for Wynona. She deserved to have the wedding that she'd admitted she had dreamed about.

It was because Clint was looking into the mirror in order to get his tie just right that he caught a glimpse of his son peering into the room. The moment Ryan realized that he'd been seen, the boy quickly stepped back, out of sight.

Clint stopped fumbling with the black fabric. The two sides of the tie hung on either side of his neck, silently mocking him.

"C'mon in, Ryan," Clint called out. "You're just the person I want to see."

"I am?" Ryan asked in unabashed surprise. The boy slowly crossed the threshold into the room and then took hesitant steps to draw closer to his father.

"Absolutely," Clint replied. He turned away from the mirror, temporarily abandoning his efforts to tie a reasonable-looking tie, and looked down at his son. "Come on over here and sit down with me, Ryan."

"Yes, sir." Ryan obediently followed him to the single small sofa in the room and sat down beside his father once the latter had taken a seat.

It occurred to Clint that the events in the past few weeks had happened very fast. When Wynona had said yes to him, he didn't want to waste any more time with things like long, formal engagements. Afraid she might change her mind or come to her senses, he was anxious to make Wynona his wife as soon as possible.

The sped-up pace was fine for him, but maybe it was a little difficult for his son to accept.

Maybe Ryan would have needed some time

to adjust to what was going on. He didn't want the boy to feel as if the rug had just been pulled out from under his feet. He was finally making amends for having ignored Ryan for all these years and he didn't want to mess it up now.

Clint put his hand on his son's shoulder and felt a twinge of guilt when he felt Ryan stiffen. The boy had turned out really well, considering how he had neglected him.

Wynona had come into *both* their lives just in time, he couldn't help thinking.

Clint left his hand on the boy's shoulder. "You okay with this?" Clint asked.

"With what?" Ryan asked almost timidly.

It occurred to Clint that he and Ryan hadn't had any father-son talks or even moments together.

He was going to have to change that. Starting now.

"With my marrying your teacher. Ms. Chee."

They were going to have to come up with a way to refer to her, Clint thought. Wynona wasn't going to just be his teacher, and calling her Mom would probably be difficult for Ryan, at least at first.

Later, Clint told himself. He'd deal with that after the wedding, not now.

"Sure," Ryan answered cheerfully. "She's great. She already told me I could call her Mom if I wanted to. And I do." He looked at his father. "Is that okay with you? 'Cause I won't if it's not," Ryan assured him quickly.

Clint slipped his arm around his son's shoulder, pulling the boy to him in a quick, impromptu hug. "It's okay with me." He felt as if he was suddenly going to choke up. "Well," he continued, taking a breath and releasing the boy, "I'd better get back to wrestling with this tie if I'm going to look presentable for this wedding."

"I can help you if you want," Ryan offered.

Clint looked at him, astonished. "You know how to tie one of these things?"

Ryan bobbed his head up and down. "Uh-huh."

"How did you learn how to do that?" Clint wanted to know, still rather skeptical that Ryan could actually live up to his claim.

"You've gotta stay sitting down or I can't reach you," Ryan said as his father began to get up. When Clint lowered himself back on the sofa, Ryan got to work. Staring intently at the tie, he quickly brought the two ends together. "Lucia taught me."

"Lucia," Clint repeated, surprised. "And why would she do that?"

"She said you never knew when something like that could come in handy." Finished, the boy beamed as he looked at his handiwork. "I guess she was right."

"I guess she was at that." Clint rose from the sofa and surveyed himself in the mirror. "Perfect," he proclaimed to his son. "So, are you ready to get married?"

Ryan beamed. "Me, too?"

"You, too," Clint answered.

Ryan slipped his small hand into his father's, his eagerness barely contained. "Let's go!"

And they did.

* * * * *

LET'S TALK

Romance

For exclusive extracts, competitions and special offers, find us online:

f facebook.com/millsandboon

⊚ @millsandboonuk

🐦 @millsandboon

Or get in touch on 0844 844 1351*

For all the latest titles coming soon, visit millsandboon.co.uk/nextmonth

Want even more
ROMANCE?

Join our bookclub today!

'Mills & Boon books, the perfect way to escape for an hour or so.'

Miss W. Dyer

'Excellent service, promptly delivered and very good subscription choices.'

Miss A. Pearson

'You get fantastic special offers and the chance to get books before they hit the shops'

Mrs V. Hall

Visit millsandbook.co.uk/Bookclub and save on brand new books.

MILLS & BOON